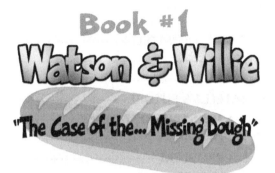

Book #1
Watson & Willie
"The Case of the... Missing Dough"

Version 11.0 – Updated, Wednesday, November 15, 2023

written by
Denny Magic

Original Soundtrack written by Tom Rae
Illustrations provided by Cyril Jordan
Audio-book narrated by Phil Williams

Get the entire 5 volume set:
"A Case of Wu Doneet"
"The Haunting of Moratuzzi Villa"
"Watson & Willie Go to America"
"The Baker "

The Original Music Soundtrack can be
streamed on **DennyMagic1.com**.

Table of Contents

INTRODUCTION

Almost three decades ago, long before I ever considered myself a writer... My late wife Nancy leaned back in her chair in our home office (that we shared in Gilroy, CA) and she suggested that because of my active imagination, that I should become a writer.

At that time, because **English 101** was <u>not</u> one of my favorite classes in High School, all I could do was laugh in disbelief at her suggestion. Up until that point the only thing that I ever wrote was a check from my bank account.

I actually laughed at her suggestion. Then I realized that she was serious.

I immediately asked her, *"What would I write?"* and she suggested that I try writing a children's book. I found her comment to be an astounding suggestion especially when I considered the fact that we didn't have children. I wondered, *'How in the heck could a guy with no kids write a children's book?'*

But... She would not 'let up' and soon I was off and running, writing my FIRST book. A Children's Story about two little Italian Mouses [sic] that can talk. YES. Book #1 in my Watson & Willie" series was the first book that I ever tried writing.

Why two Italian mouses [sic], who have the ability to speak?

Well... We had just returned from a wonderful visit to Italy on a glorious cruise ship that kept us in Europe for almost a month. The scenery was fabulous, and that particular cruise was so luxurious that we felt like royalty.

> We started out booking a very conservative room with the cruise line, but a week before our departure the company offered us a full upgrade to a 'luxurious two room suite' for a price that was definitely affordable. It was like winning the lottery.

Traveling throughout Europe (especially Italy) was nothing like I had ever imagined. I was not the world traveler that my Nancy was, and she had been after me to join her on one of her annual vacations for years.

I was not interested in a fourteen hour plane ride in 'steer-age' and some regimented planned vacation whereby you're routed from you hotel room at 7 AM every morning only to be packed up in a bus and transported to another hotel down the road.

Every time Nancy came back from one of her trips, she spent a week in bed trying to recover. *To me that was NOT 'a vacation'.* Then she suggested that we go on a cruise, and suddenly I became interested.

After that we shared a number of wonderful experiences all over the world on Cruise Ships.

You climb aboard and unpack (**once**) and you enjoy world class scenery, great food (at that time) and at the end you re-pack (a second time) and went home. I had found something that made sense... something that I came to enjoy tremendously. Suddenly I developed a new found interest in **TRAVEL**.

Getting back to the 'topic at hand' I started writing what was to become BOOK #1 - In my "Watson & Willie" series.

Nancy and I were die-hard Disney fans, and we were both enamored by **Mickey Mouse** and all the other Disney characters. We were already traveling to Anaheim, CA at least once a year to visit Disneyland.

Later, friends of ours were perplexed about our over-the-top interest in Disney, and they used to ask us... *"You don't even have kids?"* and we delighted in telling them... *"That's because, We **ARE** the kids!"*

So when I came up with the idea of two little cute, talkative mice... I decided to mold them after two comediennes who were very popular in the 1930's – **Abbott & Costello**.

I had recently watched a DVD of ***"Abbott and Costello Meet Frankenstein"*** (one of my favorite all time movies) and I decided that those two guys would serve as my benchmark for my new characters - "Watson & Willie".

When I finished Book #1 I was almost shocked that Nancy was right... I had an imagination!

Immediately I hooked up with **Amazon.com** and they helped me get my first book published.

Around that same time I met a very talented fellow engineer by the name of **Randel Chow** and we started a production company called **The Franchesa Group, Inc.**

Randel had a strong interest in music production, and together we created a brand new music publishing company. We began a search for songwriters and serendipitously we became friends with Tom Rae from Dunoon Scotland who is also a very talented songwriter, and Tom and his wife Karen seemed to love that first book of mine.

Subsequently Tom wrote a conservative six song soundtrack for **"W&W – Book #1"** (which you can stream from my website for FREE).

Since that time (almost 26 years have passed, as I write this) Tom has contributed a plethora of original music for almost all of my writing projects.   AND... he has also help recruit and coordinate other UK songwriters (as well as songwriters from all over the globe) who have made significant contributions to my original stories.

After I finished writing Book #1 I met a neighbor of mine at a *4th of July Block Party in our neighborhood* (Phil Williams) who had already narrated 46 books for **Audible.com**. Phil offered to narrate Book #1, and as a result it was my first **Audible.com** audio-book as well.

Then recently I was lucky enough to rekindle a friendship with an grammar school buddy (**Cyril Jordan**) who had become a rock & roll legend in Europe with his band ***"The Flaming Groovies"***.

I recalled that he was a great cartoonist so I asked him if he'd like to illustrate my W&W series, and much to my surprise he agreed. Book #1 is the first W&W book that he has illustrated (I know that you will appreciate his artwork) and he is currently working to illustrate the rest of the series. By the end of 2024 we have high hopes that the entire series will be illustrated.

Once Book #1 [in my "W&W" series] was written, published, and illustrated... a number of thrilled parents and grandparents began to contact me to ask when I was gonna write Book #2 ?

I was shocked beyond belief that people seemed to love the first "Watson & Willie" story that much, that they wanted more.

I considered myself lucky to have completed my first children's book and was already thinking about stopping my writing career altogether.

My confidence as a writer had not fully matured, and I was not too confident that I had made the right decision. But when the accolades started streaming in, I soon realized that *"Maybe, my wife was right? Maybe I had the makings of a writer?"*

So, I took a chance and wrote Book #2 and was also encouraged from those first editions to move forward with Book #3... and as it turned out I ended up writing five books in the "Watson & Willie" series. Trust me, I'm as amazed as you might be? I sincerely hope that you'll enjoy reading this first book to your little ones.

My last comment is that although MOST of my W&W fans are actually the adults, you will soon notice that I 'do not write down to children'. My books include a lot of 75¢ words that will force children to ask the parents and grandparents, ***"What does that mean?"***

I have no use for books that talk down to kids... *"See Jack Run... See Jack jump."* I want children to ask what certain words mean, so that there's a definite level of education woven into each of my tales. Children are extremely intelligent these days, and they don't like to be treated like little babies.

I hope that you will become fans of **Watson & Willie**, and (of course) I hope that you will want to collect all five books.

What means a lot more to me; more than selling books, is the feedback that I get from fans. Not everyone is comfortable writing a review, but... trust me... I live for the feedback and I hope that you'll use the <u>email form</u> on my website to drop me your thoughts?

So please visit my site at: <u>**DennyMagic1.com**</u> *and thank you <u>in advance</u> if you've taken a few moments to send me a review?*

Enjoy !

X

Music Track: "Giuseppe Dreams"

Home Again

Narrator:

The morning mist begins to transform itself to steam as the sun rises over the sleepy village of Moratuzzi in the lush foothills of Italy. Yet despite the early hour, Giuseppe Alessandro has already been hard at work for more than two hours – cooking up the staples that his little village has come to depend on.

You see Giuseppe is the village baker and the citizens of Moratuzzi only have Giuseppe to thank for the sweet breads, pastries, cakes, and pies that they have come to love and depend on.

Giuseppe grew up in Moratuzzi as a youngster with his father Antonio and his mother Maria, and it was there that he learned the bakery business - from his parents.

When he reached his teens, he was called into military service with the Italian Army, near the very end of world war one... and because of his baking skills... he became the baker for his regiment.

After the war Giuseppe found himself homesick for his family, and he moved back to Moratuzzi to rejoin his parents in the family business.

Unfortunately, a lot of the town's young men never returned home from the war, and many that did survive, stayed on in the countries that they were assigned to as soldiers. As a result, Moratuzzi's population became much smaller then it previously was, but this seemed to appeal to Giuseppe who had "experienced enough people" during the war.

When Giuseppe returned, he found that his parents were struggling to make ends meet - primarily because the townsfolk were busy trying to regain some sense of balance after the war, and 'normal life' had not yet returned to this close-knit community.

During his absence, and this lull in commerce... it wasn't too long before his mom and dad were forced to sell off some of the family's property in order to scale back their day-to-day existence. As his father would often say... "What were we supposed to do"?

You would think that Giuseppe would be disappointed to see his folks struggling so hard, and you might think that he would become easily bored with the lack of excitement in his sleepy little village, but over the years that followed the war, he became very close to many of the locals in this small community.

Soon he was accepted as one of their own, and the townsfolk admired him as much as they did his parents, as pillars of the community. When his mom and dad passed away, Giuseppe was faced with the dilemma of deciding if he would stay on as the town's baker - or, move on to the excitement of the big city. But after considerable thought... All he had to do was remember his war experience as a soldier in much larger cities; and he quickly decided that the experience he had come to crave was the serene countryside of his hometown... Moratuzzi.

Giuseppe also realized that once his parents passed on, his living expenses became so reasonable, that it would be very difficult for him to afford to live in a *larger Italian city. Especially if he wanted to support himself in the manner that he had become accustomed to in Moratuzzi. No, there was no chance of that now, it just wasn't a possibility.*

So as our story unfolds, Giuseppe settled into his new position as town baker, and over time he began to relish the conversational exchanges that he experienced each day with various customers who visited his bakery.

After some time had passed; Giuseppe actually started to fancy himself a sort of village celebrity, because... whenever he was seen around town, everyone seemed to know him by name, and it was likely that the people that he met on the street had enjoyed his family's bakery products at one time or another. This he thought is what made his personal investment in Moratuzzi worthwhile, and it became the primary reason why he ended up settling down in his hometown.

And then there was, Donatella

For Giuseppe, another attraction in Moratuzzi was the beautiful Donatella Figossa, heir to the Figossa Winery and Figossa Olive Oil Company.

Donatella's grandfather and grandmother had settled in the region in the late 1800's and after purchasing some of the richest mountain land... her grandfather began to plant grape vines, and olive trees.

The olive trees thrived, and produced enough olive oil that the family was able to afford to add to the size of their vineyards, and as a result... The Figossa's became one of the largest landowners in the region, and, one of the largest suppliers of olive oil in the world.

The winery never really caught on with the rest of the world, but they had certainly conquered Italy itself, and made a respectable living from wine sales all over the local region.

Because Donatella's father was Swiss, she did not have the usual olive colored skin that most people from Moratuzzi sported, even though her mother Luisa was 100% Italian and a native of Moratuzzi.

Instead, Donatella was about as fair skinned as one could imagine, and this reminded Giuseppe of the beautiful European women he had seen when he was on active duty as a soldier.

Giuseppe was struck by Donatella's simplistic beauty, but he was also in constant denial that she would ever take any interest in a lowly baker. With her family's wealth and her educated upbringing, Giuseppe thought that it was unlikely that she would ever fall for him.

It was also common knowledge that a local boy Anthony Stabenelli had his eyes focused firmly on Donatella, and this added to Giuseppe's pessimism that he would ever connect with Donatella. He realized early on that his chances were slim at best.

Anthony's family was a significant part of the Italian Marble Business in the region. They exported marble slabs that were used in buildings all over Europe, and his father had recently traveled to America to make arrangements to sell the family's marble in that growing country - as well.

Besides, it didn't take much of an imagination for Giuseppe to imagine Anthony and Donatella together because both their families were wealthy, and they just seemed to go together so well... Even Giuseppe had to admit that.

Yet the thought of loving Donatella continued to haunt Giuseppe, like a ghost that would not go away. And Anthony, well... Giuseppe seemed to find everything that was wrong with him, so it was easy for him to dislike this rival for Donatella's affections.

For one, Anthony was quite the braggart, and he frequently flaunted his family's wealth around the town, showing off whenever he could... As an example, he was the second citizen in Moratuzzi to actually own an automobile after the war, and it didn't take him long to convince Donatella to join him for elaborate car rides all over the Italian countryside. This activity irked Giuseppe, and he often had to remind himself that Donatella was not **his** girlfriend, and that he had to keep his emotions under control.

But to Giuseppe, it soon became obvious that Anthony wanted nothing more than to leave this sleepy little backwoods community and venture out to some big city where he could feed his need for a flamboyant lifestyle. He wondered if Donatella had the same aspirations, or... was she the kind of girl who wanted to settle down and raise a family?

Once he decided; entirely on his own, that Donatella wanted to become a homemaker... He speculated that her future interest in Anthony would wane, and it was these types of thoughts that gave Giuseppe false hopes.

Anthony was too young when world war one started, so he never had to serve, which initially gave him very little opportunity to travel far from Moratuzzi... This Giuseppe surmised would stifle his experience in the world.

Because Anthony lacked the worldly experience that Giuseppe had gained, he reasoned that if Donatella knew this, she would begin to see right through Anthony's worldly deceptions.

However, Giuseppe continued to deceive himself by fantasizing that he'd sweep Donatella off her feet and make her his wife. He might not be wealthy, but he reasoned that he had become a pillar of the community, someone who could be trusted... and Donatella would someday discover this about him.

But he also was aware that Anthony was probably filling Donatella's head with promises that he'd whisk her away to some far off places in elaborate cities. Places where he could monopolize her attentions exclusively for himself. Yikes! Giuseppe thought... *"I have to get a hold of my imagination before I drive myself crazy."* He thought.

Occasionally when Giuseppe visited other shops in the village and took the time to make conversation with the local townsfolk, he would hint about his affection for Donatella. This was his way of trying to communicate his feelings to Donatella. He thought that some of the villagers might convey his feelings to her on his behalf, when they saw Donatella, like school children often do.

At least this was his plan, when he telegraphed his feelings for the girl to any townsfolk that would listen to his pipedreams. He even thought, most townsfolk already knew Anthony for the braggart that he was, and he wondered why Donatella couldn't see this for herself.

Anyway, despite the reality of the situation, Giuseppe dreamed that one day Donatella would choose him instead of Anthony and become Mrs. Alessandro. As long as that thought remained a priority in Giuseppe's mind, it was unlikely that he would ever consider leaving Moratuzzi.

Despite Giuseppe's 'visions of grandeur' he tried his best to keep his intentions mostly to himself - longing for the affections of Donatella quietly in the background.

More times than he would have liked - reality would set in when Anthony would come into the bakery to order some expensive cake for one of his family's extravagant parties to be held at their hill top villa.

Without trying, Anthony seemed to reek of ostentatious behavior, including that <u>fake</u> English accent, which really irked Giuseppe.

As if the situation regarding Donatella and Anthony wasn't enough; Giuseppe hated it when Anthony would bring his stinky little English bulldog 'Spike', who would drool all over his clean floors.

The bottom line was, Giuseppe disliked that dog almost as much as he disliked Anthony; in fact, he even hated that specific breed of dog... The drool, the mean scowl on that dog's face, the dog's personality, and nervous ticks, and even the dog's odor all ensured that this animal was not high on Giuseppe's list of 'favorite things in life'.

Not to mention that Spike had a suspicious personality, and always seemed to be thinking, ***"I know something is wrong in here and I'm gonna find out what it is!"***

Nothing about Anthony's dog appealed to Giuseppe, and because that demon monster seemed to be connected to the hip of Anthony Stabenelli, it made things seem evermore worse for Giuseppe.

However, Giuseppe was reluctant to say anything derogatory about Spike, which might upset Anthony. He kept his comments to himself and a smile on his face, because Anthony was always spending large sums of money in the bakery, and frankly, Giuseppe wanted his business.

This experience was truly painful for Giuseppe because Anthony [being the braggart that he was] would always describe each and every grand event that his family was hosting at their villa. He seemed to think that all Giuseppe had to do all day was sit around listening to Anthony brag.

10

Anthony was always quick to explain how much money his family was going to spend on each planned event, He even gave details about the number of servants who would work that night, and in some cases Anthony would go on and on about how many presents that his family would be providing to their guests.

You see, being invited to a party at the Stabenelli's Villa was quite a privilege, and most guests would be clamoring for an invitation just to see what kind of gifts they could go home with. In a sense, Giuseppe saw this as a way that the Stabenelli's could "Buy" their friendships. So, in Giuseppe's mind, he reasoned that these parties at the Stabenelli's were not something he would normally approve of.

However, once Giuseppe calmed down and started to think rationally, he always laughed at his own jealousy, and somewhat irrational thoughts. Then when he was just beginning to think of Anthony as a regular human being... Anthony would always add fuel to the fire.

Suddenly Anthony would justify the decision to spend a fortune, by making sure that Giuseppe was educated about the quality of each event, and he would point out that his family always selected the best of everything when it came to gifts.

Then he'd pause for effect... and say, *"But you already know that we only buy the best, which explains why we get all our baked goods from you, right?"*

Even as Giuseppe tried to show his appreciation for Anthony's repeated business, by praising his family's good judgment... Anthony always seemed to remain highly critical of anything Giuseppe provided to the conversation as if to 'shut-him-up'.

For example, when Giuseppe would try to make some helpful suggestion... Anthony was always quick to point out why that suggestion wouldn't work, or that, *"They'd already tried that once in the past, and that idea failed."*

Every suggestion was followed with criticism and a comment like, *"No, that won't work... We already learned our lesson the hard-way about that."*

If anyone could irritate Giuseppe more than Anthony, Giuseppe had not met that person. Then to put the icing on the cake... Anthony would go on by naming all the celebrities and politicians that would be coming from Venice and Rome, which sometimes included movie stars like the young and beautiful Sophia Loren.

Once he even claimed that actor Charlie Chaplin was on the family's guest list. That's what really made these visits by Anthony really irritating. All Giuseppe could do was bite his lip and smile. He'd tell himself to act pleasant, and in the end, just take Anthony's order.

Despite the financial benefits of Anthony's visits to the bakery, all of them seemed to end up setting Giuseppe's attitude for the day several steps behind. And the really depressing part of the day was when the conversation would turn to how close Anthony was to winning Donatella's heart. Sometimes Giuseppe just wanted to scream.

He often felt defeated because he knew that Anthony had piles of money to buy Donatella's affections, and all he could do was hold onto hope that Donatella would eventually see how shallow Anthony was.

Giuseppe occasionally saw Donatella downtown and one day she and he caught each other's eye; and she actually smiled at him... As a result, Giuseppe ended up whistling in pure joy for more than a week.

Most of his customers and the villagers thought that he'd flipped his noodle, but as always... a visit from Anthony brought him back down to earth.

Despite the setbacks... Giuseppe seemed determined to break free of his shyness with women and he made a personal vow to himself to speak to Donatella, before... [He reasoned] Anthony could propose to her, and spoil Giuseppe's dreams.

Yet he instinctively seemed to understand that once Anthony became aware of his interest in Donatella, it was likely that he'd lose the Stabenelli family as one of his best customers.

What a dilemma, what a dilemma indeed.

The Secret's Out!

What began as just another wonderful day in Moratuzzi was set off kilter when Giuseppe heard the little bell on his bakery's front door, which was usually a sign that a customer had entered his shop.

Immediately he dropped everything; and made haste to get from the back room where 'the magic' took place, to the front part of his little shop where he sold his wares.

Unfortunately, there in all his glory, stood his nemesis (Anthony) with that horrible Spike under his arm. He mustered up a false smile and greeted Anthony (and Spike) as if Anthony was his best customer and Spike his favorite dog. In reality, Anthony probably did

14

spend the most money in the bakery, when compared to all of Giuseppe's other customers.

Giuseppe understood that Anthony spent enough in his little shop, that without his business, he would not have learned so much about being the master baker that he had become. For that alone, he was somewhat indebted to Anthony, as Anthony's money had helped finance his education over the past few years, allowing him to experiment with innovative baking ideas.

Yet no amount of money could mask the hidden animosities that Giuseppe felt for this man. There were just too many irritating characteristics he associated with Anthony to overcome this aversion.

For instance, something that really irritated Giuseppe about Anthony was that he somehow got it into his mind that in order to be sophisticated, he needed to absorb everything he could that was English.

His fancy car was from England, his clothing was imported from London, even his bull dog was English, and as phony as it all was... Anthony had even adapted an English accent, which he fancied as the 'frosting on the cake', no pun intended.

To Giuseppe, Anthony's fake accent really was ridiculous, especially when combined with his stereotypical Italian gestures, and his unmistakable

Italian accent that crept in to every other word that Anthony spoke.

Anthony's accent bothered Giuseppe almost as much as his filthy little mutt, which Anthony dragged around town with him - day in, and day out.

Giuseppe often wondered how Donatella could stand that poor excuse of a dog, and he shuttered to himself when he thought of Anthony and Donatella trying to go somewhere on a picnic together with that drooling mutt on the front seat of the car.

Anyway, business was business, and Giuseppe did his best to hide all of his personal thoughts, while dealing with Anthony as a regular customer.

"Good morning Giuseppe" Anthony said, in the worst fake English accent that you've ever heard.

"Good Morning Anthony... How can I help you?" asked Giuseppe.

Anthony replied... *"My eh family has decided to throw a little get together in two weeks on Saturday, and as usual I have been delegated the responsibility of acquiring the desserts. This time, I wondered if you were up for the task of creating something unusual in a cake?"*

Giuseppe knew that Anthony was well aware that Giuseppe was a master baker when it came to creating innovative cakes, but this predictable banter had almost become routine, whenever Anthony came in.

What went on was like a little 'dance' that the two men seemed to engage in every time Anthony showed up. Even though Giuseppe detested this banter, he did use the time wisely to size up Anthony, as he evaluated him as 'the competition'.

He reasoned that if he were ever to have the slightest chance of winning Donatella's heart... he would have to be very well educated about who his competition was, including how Anthony's mind worked.

This day was a bit different though, because as Anthony set his bulldog on the floor beside him, the dog took notice of some movement just to the left-hand side of the glass showcase.

Spike immediately set his stumpy legs into high gear, and as they began to spin on Giuseppe's slick hardwood floor, Spike was building up momentum to take off like a rocket.

Luckily Anthony had his monster's leash attached to Spike's collar, and when the dog took off to run behind the counter, Anthony stepped down to pinch the leash to the floor, which effectively stopped Spike in his tracks.

Anthony wrestled the dog back to his side of the showcase and picked him back up as if he were a little baby child. Giuseppe did his best not to gag, as drool from this beast seemed to splatter all over his clean hardwood floors and the glass on his showcase. Yuk!

Unfortunately, there was no time for Giuseppe to intervene to stop this incident, and as he stepped around the showcase to offer a helping hand to Anthony, he could see that Anthony's composure was disheveled. He seemed embarrassed that Giuseppe had to see him off kilter, as he struggled back to his feet with the pudgy Spike under his left arm.

 "Giuseppe, are you aware that you have a mouse in your bakery!" ... He shouted.

Anthony's comment seemed more like an accusation against Giuseppe's character, rather than a helpful tip from a Good Samaritan.

When Giuseppe didn't respond immediately... Anthony added, *"I certainly hope to God that you keep a sanitary work space back there"* as he pointed with his free hand towards the business end of the bakery. *"I mean, my family wouldn't want anything connected to a mice infestation to end up in our cake"*.

Giuseppe shook his head as if to try and reassure him, then he stated with authority, *"No, no... This is a new problem, and I can assure you that I have already taken eh steps to alleviate it... besides...*

18

it's only one mouse, and it's the first one that we have had in many, many years. It's certainly no infestation, I can assure you."

Anthony looked on silently for a long moment at Giuseppe, as he gave him the evil eye, and then he finally seemed to accept his answer as fact. *"OK then. I think I'll take my little buddy for a romp in the park."* Anthony then broke out in a sort of broken baby talk, with that very poor English accent, as he spoke directly to Spike, *"Would my little buddy like to go to the parky poo?"*

OH, No, Not A Cat!

Meanwhile from our point of view, we find ourselves looking out into the bakery from the inside of a relatively small, half-round, mouse hole... Here comes a mouse; running at full speed, clamoring to get to the safety of this sanctuary.

He entered his little house, slammed the door, and skidded to a stop. He put his back against the door with outstretched limbs.

Obviously he's out of breath, and visibly shaken.

Without looking up from his book, comes the voice of reason, *"Willie. What did you do now?"*

There - sitting on a padded spool of thread - is Watson, who was lazily reading a book when Willie made his grand entrance.

An out of breath Willie answers, *"Nothing, I wasn't doing anything Watson, I swear".*

Watson smugly responded, *"Uh huh. So, what were you doing in the bakery during the day, when you were supposedly doing nothing? I thought we agreed that we would avoid the bakery during the day?"*

Willie is obviously caught red handed. *"OK, OK. I was looking for something fresh to eat. I get tired of eating all those day old, crumbs. That showcase has the real good stuff in it, and you know it!"* ...Willie explained.

We watch as Willie hopped over to the edge of Watson's giant book, and Watson got up to turn the page. *"Willie look, our very existence depends on our ability to remain unseen, especially while the bakery is open for business. Giuseppe is so busy working during the day, he isn't aware that we existed until you started venturing out, sneaking food at all hours of the day. Besides, just look how fat you're getting. It seems like you're eating all the time now!"*

Willie shrugged his shoulders; turning towards a little cosmetic hand-mirror that the two of them have propped up, against the wall. He looks over his somewhat chubby shape and slides his hands up and down his waist in a very vane manner. Then he gets that, *'I've been caught'* look, on his face, and responded, **"Giuseppe didn't see me."**

Watson looks a bit disappointed and says, **"Even if Giuseppe didn't actually see you himself, that customer probably did, and that's my point."**

Willie interrupts, **"It was Anthony Stabenelli, and he didn't see me, it was his stinky little mutt, Spike that caught a quick glimpse of me."**

Watson sits up and places his hands on his hips and says, **"Willie, the bottom line is that Anthony, Giuseppe and Spike are all aware of you <u>now</u>, and this is exactly what I've been trying to avoid. Next thing you know Giuseppe will be getting himself a cat, and then what? We've got a pretty good thing going on here, and I don't want to mess it up!"**

A Cat?

Willie realizes his mistake and shakes his head from side to side, **"Alright, I get it. First comes a cat, and then we have to find a new place to live. Right?"**

"OK Then. I'm glad that you're listening to me for a change" ... Watson tries to relax and takes his seat, getting back to his book. **"You know if you're bored... you could take up reading. Giuseppe has quite a library upstairs, and I'd be willing to borrow a book for you once in a while, and you might even learn something."**

23

Willie makes a face, **"Reading isn't my thing, I'm more of an action mouse. I live for the thrill of conquest, the adventure, the chase..."**

For emphasis Watson casually adds, **"The Cat."**

Without thinking Willie continues reciting his list and unknowingly adds, **"The Cat".** Realizing his mistake, **"No, no, I didn't mean to say that! Not The Cat".**

Willie leans over to the book Watson is reading, and asks, **"So, what you reading this time?"**

"This is a recipe book for bakers." he says without even looking up.

Willie looks a bit perplexed, and asks, **"So, what... if I may be so bold as to ask, are you reading that for? You trying to become a baker?"**

It's obvious Watson hates to have to explain himself to Willie, and he looks at him, as if thinking, OK. Here we go again. **"Well... I figure the more finished products that we chew on at night; the easier it will be for Giuseppe to figure out that we might be a problem. If we can focus on eating the ingredients, before they become tasty cakes, pies, and pastries... the less chance Giuseppe will be reminded that we might be here."**

Willie looks up into the air exasperated, shakes his head, and says, **"Well that's no fun. I can't**

24

*imagine chewing on a mouth full of dough...
yuck!"*

Watson stares at his partner for a brief moment, then
answers, *"Why, it's the same ingredient that
goes into one of Giuseppe's golden loaves of
French bread. And besides, there are wonderful
ingredients like fruits and berries that taste
great long before they're turned into delicious
desserts. What's wrong with those?"*

Willie smirks. *"Yeah, but... they don't taste as
good as Giuseppe's custard, or that luscious
meringue he comes up with for his pies."*

Watson stands up and points to the mirror, *"Yeah, I
can't argue with that, but take a quick look in
the mirror again, to see what that custard is
doing to your belly!"*

Willie sneaks a peak towards the mirror and gets a
defiant look on his face, and says, *"Did you know
that a mirror could add twenty pounds to the
way you look?"*

Music Track: "Dolce Vita"

25

Discussing Donatella's Future

It's a beautiful spring morning here in the foothills of Moratuzzi, and the scenery is especially picturesque at the Figossa Winery as we see Donatella working alongside her mother in the family's winery. She pauses for a moment from watching the birds, and takes a long hard look at her mom, and then bursts out, *"Mama"* she asks, *"How old were you, when you and papa became married?"*

Donatella's mother smiles knowing that this conversation was long overdue, and she replies, *"Why? Are you thinking about getting married?"* and her mother chuckles to herself, knowing full well the answer that's coming.

"No mama" Donatella answers immediately, *"But I'm starting to grow up, and these things are becoming a curiosity to me, besides, you have more experience in these matters."*

Donatella's mother appreciates that her daughter trusts her enough to even ask her opinion, and she gets back to her task as she tries to offer good motherly advice in her answer, *"I think that you're kind of young to be thinking about that right now. Don't you?"*

Donatella laughs. *"Of course, mama, I just want to be mentally prepared; when and if, the*

26

situation comes up. I mean, that will be one of the most important things in my life, right? And I should have a good idea what to do when the situation comes along. Right?"

Her mother smiles at her daughter's intellectual approach, knowing that she must have brought her up correctly, especially if she is so confident to come to her mother. *"Well... Your father and I were married when we were very young, maybe too young... Ahhhh, but we were so in love."*

Her mom seems to drift off into a fantasy for a brief moment, then she regains her composure. *"Each individual must weigh the circumstances, there is no right or wrong answer, and I suspect that when you meet the right person, you will know when the time is right."*

Donatella's mom stares at her daughter for a moment. *"Is this about that Anthony Stabenelli?"*

Donatella snaps back from her own deep thoughts. *"No, of course not. Besides I already know that papa doesn't like Anthony."*

"Oh, my goodness." she walks over to her daughter. *"When you meet the right person, it won't matter if your papa, or me, approves of*

your choice. Your heart must help you make that decision."

Donatella gets an inquisitive look on her face. *"But it's going to be important to get papa's approval, and if he doesn't like the man I select..."*

Donatella's mother smiles. *"Look I am going to tell you something, when my father met your papa for the first time he did not care for him either. It took time for grandpa to see the talent and determination that your father had. And it's a good thing that he did, because..."* she gestures with her hand as if to paint a glorious picture of their land. *"All of this came about because your papa had a vision. So, it's important to look deep within a person to see their future potential."* She paused for a moment while Donatella seemed to be soaking everything up. *"However, I am not saying that Anthony Stabenelli has the same qualities that your papa has."* She resumed her work.

Donatella stops, as she tries to find hidden meanings in her mother's words of wisdom. *"So, you're saying that you don't like Anthony either?"*

"No, I didn't say that!" her mother instantly replied. *"I'm not telling you that at all, I am just saying that what will be, will be, and in the end,*

28

it will have to be your decision. Besides, are we talking about Anthony here?"

Donatella smirks and gets back to work. *"No. Not really. I'm not getting serious about anyone yet. In fact, I'm a bit curious about another young man in town."* She pauses. *"But I'm not serious about him either, I'm just wondering a little, I can wonder can't I?"*

"And who might that other man be, if you don't mind me asking?" her mother asks.

Donatella answers reluctantly. *"Giuseppe Alessandro."*

Her mother raises her eyebrows in surprise, *"Giuseppe the Baker?"*

The Baker?

Donatella stops working, and stares back at her mother. **"Yes, the baker, what's wrong with that?"**

Donatella's mother realizes that she has been attempting to give her daughter the personal freedom to make choices for herself, and now she realizes that all of a sudden she is trying to influence her unnecessarily. She paused for a moment while she considers her words carefully. **"Is he nice?"**

Donatella instantly replies with enthusiasm, **"I really don't know him as well as I'd like to. He seems** nice, but he seems a little bit shy, and, we've never spoken except in his bakery."

She stops to ponder the situation. *"According to the people in the village, he's a hard worker, and very well thought of in the community, and everyone knows that he makes some of the most wonderful desserts in the whole world."*

Her mother smiles and nods in agreement and says, *"I just love those little lemon tarts that he makes."*

Donatella is surprised that her mom has drifted away from the conversation to Giuseppe's Lemon Tarts. So, she tries to get the conversation back on track, *"But Anthony's family has money, like us."*

Her mother laughs out loud. *"Yes, at least that's what he loves to tell everyone, and if it's true, and I would suspect that it probably is... that's probably the one thing that your papa would like about him. But in life, there are a lot more important things than money."*

Donatella frowns. *"Like What?"*

Her mom bends over to hoist a bushel basket to the wagon that she is working next to. *"Like Love"*

She pauses and stares at Donatella for a brief moment, *"This could be the most important decision that you make in your life, and you*

31

surely don't want it to be based upon how much money someone has, right?"

Donatella hoists her own bushel basket next to the one that her mom just lifted. Then she glares at her mother, *"Ah ha! So, it's true... you and papa don't like Anthony."*

Her mother's eyes roll up in her head and she replies, *"I did not say that. I married your papa because I loved him, not because he was rich. That's all I'm saying."* She paused and then reached out to touch Donatella's hand. *"In the end, it has to be your decision. But whatever you decide, you'll have to live with it."*

Donatella smiles, and then walks away to resume her work.

Music Track: "Delivery Day"

A Lot of Dough, Earns Lots of Money

Giuseppe is without a doubt, a very hard worker. He's up before dawn each and every day, when he heads downstairs to his little bakery from his living quarters above the store, to begin his work.

Bread is naturally a priority, seeing as this is one of the staples of life for the entire village. With quite a large number of loaves being baked weekly. Each day's rations are ready to go by 11 am, Giuseppe is lucky to have several local young people who come around on their bicycles, who are willing to make bread deliveries to Giuseppe's established list of longtime customers. This is an important part of his business as it serves as the main cash flow for his company.

Every Monday the delivery of the raw bakery ingredients that he will use during his busy workweek arrives. This is a very important event that sets the pace for the entire week.

That's why this interruption [in his busy schedule] is a necessary evil, as he has to set aside time to work with some of the delivery trucks that come between 9am and noon. With this added responsibility, Monday's are very hectic to be sure.

This is why a major effort goes into baking up loaves of fresh bread and having them ready to deliver by the time the kids start showing up on their bicycles. When everything happens correctly, Giuseppe's bakery operation runs like a Swiss watch, and [lucky for him] the majority of weeks get off to a good start.

In addition to deliverymen showing up, and kids showing up around the same time to make a few liras [delivering fresh bread] there is always the errant customer that comes in early, and for them he has to have his showcases filled with at least a portion of the day's fresh loaves.

Thankfully most customers are experienced enough to know that Monday mornings the bakery will <u>not</u> have a stockpile of cakes, cupcakes, pies, cookies, and pastries to choose from.

For those early birds, Giuseppe usually tries to have an assortment of bagels, which *usually* satisfy the diehards, at least until he can flex his culinary muscles later on in the week.

Thanks to his parents who established the baking patterns that Giuseppe follows to this day, the old time customers have become accustomed to the availability of baked goods in Moratuzzi, and for the most part they know what they can expect Tuesdays through Saturdays.

However, occasionally a new face pops in the bakery on a Monday, wondering where all the other stuff is? However, if they aren't a 'one-time tourist', Giuseppe simply reminds them about his schedule, and suggests that they come back tomorrow.

As his customer base expanded over the years, it has become apparent that he could use another baker, or [at the very least] a counter person to handle sales.

When the frustration seems to mount, Giuseppe will simply pause for a moment and 'give thanks' that he not only has a job... but that he is thriving while still being his own boss.

The other good news is that many of the deliverymen have been coming to the bakery since his parents ran the business. For those seasoned men, Giuseppe musters up a smile and a wave, and for the most part, they have free reign to operate on their own in the bakery.

Each of them knows the layout of the bakery as well as Giuseppe, and some of them, he hardly notices when they come or go. Usually they are in-and-out, so quickly; it's like they were not even there.

Yet, he is often surprised, because he discovers that his cooler and shelves are magically stocked up for the week, with everything in its proper place.

Giuseppe is a member of the Baker's Guild and receives a newsletter each week from Rome. This he reads at night; from cover to cover, for inside information about the baking business. He especially loves to review the new recipes that he often tries out on his own customers.

His customers often read about exotic desserts in magazines that they subscribe to, which feature great recipes from Rome, and even France, and in many cases, Giuseppe already has one or more of those fancy desserts in his showcase by the end of each week.

This he reasons, is why he has such a loyal following. People just know that Giuseppe will work hard to stay on top of all the latest trends. They can count on him.

In reality this attention to detail, which is also paid-attention-to by several of the other merchants in town... is probably why Moratuzzi is such a close-knit community with up to date trends.

Customers realize that they don't have to travel all the way to Rome to taste the latest in culinary delights, or purchase the latest fashions, because the local merchants [for the most part] really do pay attention to the rest of the world.

Once a month the merchants get together after church and discuss how they can improve their services for the community, and this extra effort has really paid off for all of them.

In fact, within the last few years Moratuzzi has started to attract its own tourists. Imagine that; tourists who have come to visit Moratuzzi?

Nearby lake Talaaz offers paddle boat rentals, and the new *Moratuzzi Inn* opened just a year before, which features many of Giuseppe's artisan breads and desserts for their guests. Yes. All in all, life is good... and once in a while Giuseppe stops to think about how lucky he really is.

Moratuzzi Grows

When Giuseppe's parents ran the business, the surrounding area was full of open fields that provided great access to the few buildings in town for all the wildlife, including the mice. Once Giuseppe's parents realized that they had a problem, they acquired a great big old tomcat and he [mostly] took care of the mouse issues, at least when he wasn't lounging around the bakery.

38

Suddenly they didn't have a problem anymore. But about the same time that Giuseppe returned from the war, the cat wandered away, and of course even before that happened... scores of new buildings went up, in a small but significant construction boom. Construction pushed back the open fields away from town, and even though the bakery didn't have the luxury of its own cat for several years after Giuseppe's return... The mice seemed to stay away... At least until now.

Giuseppe had thought that he'd seen signs of mice, but there was nothing he could really identify as a real problem. Moving scores of bakery goods around the shop from showcase to showcase would cause some goods to lose a corner of their form in such a way as to imply that they may have become lunch for some hungry mouse. But in reality he just wasn't sure. At least not until Anthony's mutt 'Spike' had lunged towards that mouse [Willie] the other day.

Giuseppe hadn't seen the mouse himself, so he had to listen to Anthony's comments about what he thought he had seen. Regardless, the idea had already crossed his mind and he did recall telling himself 'Next week - he'd look into the matter.' However, a nagging voice in the back of his mind, told him not to believe anything that Anthony said, and lord knows that he could not use Anthony's dog as a validation that he had a mouse problem. However, the thought was planted and... 'Next Week' he'd look into getting a cat.

A Cat Would be a Problem

Around 8:30 or 9:00 am Watson and Willie both began to stir from bed. Willie barely woke up at all, but when he did raise his head; he looked at Watson for a brief moment, then he fell over and promptly went back to sleep.

Watson, who was much more of a responsible mouse, stood up and stretched, and then pulled off his nightcap and pajamas and slipped into his regular clothes. He was careful to make the bed, and fold his pajamas, setting them out neatly on the bed, for the next time.

Adjacent to their bedroom was the area set aside for their kitchen, and when Watson walked into it, he was greeted with a pile of dirty dishes that Willie had left from the night before. Willie and Watson had an arrangement [sort of] that when there was cooking to do, Watson would be the culinary artist, and afterwards Willie would do the cleanup.

Watson shook his head somewhat disappointed at the habits of his 'not so dependable' roommate, but just like he always did, he went ahead and cleaned up the mess. He spoke out loud to himself, ***"The things I do for you Willie!"***

C.J.

At the mention of his name, Willie stirred; he lifted his half-asleep head, and mumbled, ***"Huh?"***

Watson took one quick glance back over his shoulder, to his sleeping buddy, and waved his hand and said, ***"Nothing. Go back to sleep."***

The day was rather routine. Willie finally awoke around 10 am and immediately rubbed his hands together and headed towards the kitchen to eat.

Watson was enjoying a thimble full of Earl Grey Tea as he brought Willie to a complete stop with his outstretched hand.

Willie asked, **"What?"**

Watson, merely pointed towards the washbasin, and Willie understood that once again he was forgetting an important step. Like 'Washing your paws before you eat'.

As long as Watson was standing guard, Willie knew that he had to wash up first, especially if he ever expected to have his breakfast. It was a simple chore, but Willie always made a fuss to indicate that he wasn't happy jumping through the hoops that Watson was always imposing onto his bohemian lifestyle.

When Willie returned to the kitchen, Watson said, **"We need to talk."**

Willie [of course] assumed that the upcoming conversation would be about his lack of etiquette, so he chimed in, saying, **"OK. Tomorrow I'll wash up before I come in to eat."**

Watson started to shake his head no because that isn't what he wanted to talk about. He had a little piece of pastry in his mouth, that he wasn't quite finished chewing on, so he covers his mouth for an extra second or two, speaking through his open paw, **"No, no. It's not about that."**

Willie took a seat on a spool of thread and slid it up closer to the table to listen, and Watson stood up and began to pace. **"Yesterday's incident was a real wake up call. Do you remember the stories that we heard from all the older mice about the monster that used to live here in the bakery?"**

He stumbles for the right words. **"That beast. That creature. That killer, yeah I think that was his name... Killer!"** He shakes his head as if pondering the tall tales that his predecessors had told him. **"We don't want Giuseppe getting another cat like Killer."**

Willie is nodding in agreement and occasionally blurts out a supportive comment as Watson spins his tale. **"I can't agree with you more Watson."**

Watson stops talking and stares at Willie for a moment, as if he feels that his interruptions are meaningless. **"OK. Look. As long as we're both in agreement about that, we'll have to figure out a way to turn our situation around so that Giuseppe thinks of us as a favorable addition, and not 'the enemy'."**

Willie smacks himself in the forehead and shakes his head no. **"We're mouses [sic], we ARE the**

43

enemy! We're vermin that the humans always want to get rid of. How are we going to change Giuseppe's opinion of us?"

Watson stops pacing and takes a seat. *"Well, that my furry friend, is the dilemma that we are faced with. We need to come up with some solution so that we can continue to live here without fear."*

Willie adopts a look of concern and begins to rub his chin, as if he's trying to come up with a solution. Watson knows that he means well but does not expect any great revelations to come from the snout of Willie.

Everything is Ship Shape

As the end of another long day comes to a close, Giuseppe waits on his last customer, Mrs. De Stefano. He fishes out a great big chocolate chip cookie with a piece of tissue, and hands it to the sweet old lady. *"Here ya go Francine, here's a little something for your son Frankie."*

Mrs. De Stefano who is about twice Giuseppe's age (at least) flutters her eyelashes at him and smiles affectionately, **"Why thank you Giuseppe, you're such a gentleman, I wish I could find myself a nice man like you, to spend the autumn of my life with. And maybe that son of mine would finally get a job and move out."**

Not wanting to launch the same old story he's heard fifty times before, Giuseppe does his best to bite his tongue, only nodding and smiling in agreement.

Mrs. De Stefano smiles back and can see that Giuseppe isn't interested in hearing about her son again. **"Yes, well... I guess I better get on my way before it gets too dark. Until next time Giuseppe... Ciao."**

Giuseppe gives her a friendly wave and then follows her to the door of the bakery, where he gently locks the latch. 'Ahhhh' he thinks to himself... Finally.'

Now starts the hour [or so] process of closing up the bakery, and cleaning everything so it's just right for the next day.

Giuseppe puts everything in its proper place, then comes the sweeping and mopping of the floors, and finally the cleaning of the glass showcases from all the fingerprints left by the children of his customers. He thinks to himself, how valuable these kids are to his business. He ponders that they are, in essence, like little salesmen.

While their parents are selecting the staples of life, such as artisan breads, the kids spend their time staring at all the fancy pastries in the showcases and then each of them, using their own 'powers of persuasion', end up persuading their parents to buy cupcakes, cookies, and Danish style pastries.

So, a showcase full of fingerprints at the end of each workday is a small price to pay for the mountain of goods that Giuseppe sells on a regular basis.

Once those kids grow up and get married, a whole new generation of hungry munchkins will take their place.

Giuseppe gives his little bakery the final check, and once convinced that everything is in ship shape. he sighs, takes off his baker's apron, hanging it up on a hook on the wall. Then he makes his way around to the front of the showcases, and over to a little stairway that leads upstairs to his second floor apartment where he lives.

It's a long and narrow set of stairs, and Giuseppe is a bit worn out after his long day, so he methodically takes each step one at a time, almost like the ticking of an old clock, the sound of his footsteps fade, when he nears the top landing.

Patience My Good Man, Patience

Willie is watching Watson standing at the front door of their mouse-house, and Watson is watching Giuseppe who begins walking up that long flight of stairs. **"Is he gone yet?"** prods Willie

Watson is a bit perturbed by Willie's lack of patience, and he spins around with his claw in front of his snout, **"Shush"** he says... **"Keep your voice down. Be as quiet as a church mouse."**

Willie chimes in, **"But this is a bakery!"**

Watson says, **"Never mind."**

He adds, **"Patience my good man, patience. Remember, patience is a virtue."**

Willie hates it when Watson starts babbling his fancy sayings. Things that he's obviously learned from reading books. Willie questions, **"What's that supposed to mean?"**

Watson ponders the explanation that he's about to give, so as not to confuse Willie too much with intellectual banter, **"Well, it's like this. When you** *rush into something too fast, mistakes can happen. Like when you rushed into the bakery before it was closed. Remember that? You almost got caught, right?"*

Willie actually seems to be getting this, and he nods yes, so Watson continues, *"And if you got caught, I would have surely been discovered as well, and this little piece of paradise would have been no more."* He pauses for a moment to let things soak in.

Once Willie starts to nod that he understands, Watson continues, *"Had you followed the established plan, you would not have had a close call, and Giuseppe wouldn't be thinking about getting a cat, right? You didn't think things through because you could not wait to eat, you were impatient."*

Willie seems to understand the trouble he may have caused.   He inquires, *"So, patience is waiting?"* Watson tries a slightly different approach. *"Thinking things through before you make snap decisions prevents potential problems, and it's that ability, that shows that you have patience."*

Willie is feeling ever so slightly remorseful again, for his recent dumb decision, and he says, *"I said I was sorry."*

Watson walks over and puts his paw around Willie's shoulder. *"Hey, I know that you're sorry Willie, and everyone makes mistakes, all I'm staying is, we need to have a little more patience, and maybe we can avoid mistakes altogether, OK?"*

Willie nods, and asks, *"So, when can we eat?"*

Watson smiles and says, *"As soon as you hear Giuseppe start snoring, we're free to hit the smorgasbord."*

At the top of the stairs, as the door to Giuseppe's apartment gently closes with a loud click. The boys realize that this is what they've been waiting for. This is the sound that Watson was listening for as the <u>first</u> indicator. He smiles, and turning towards Willie saying, *"OK. Let's give Giuseppe a few more minutes to settle in."* Willie is very anxious as he is every night, and gets a very disappointed look on his face, "*Come on Watson. He ain't coming back downstairs, he never does!"*

"And if he does? Then what? That's when the new cat will show up right on schedule!" Watson warns.

"Cats... That's all I hear about these days is cats... I'm so hungry! In fact, I could probably eat a cat!" exclaims Willie.

49

Willie's complaining, or his attempt at humor doesn't break Watson's concentration from the sanctuary of their mouse house, as he stares out into the empty bakery. ***"Patience my good man, patience."***

Giuseppe's Sanctuary

As Giuseppe closes the door to his apartment he pauses and stands there for a moment taking in the view of his sanctuary, above the bakery. It's not much, but it's all his.

He sighs and makes his way over to a little round table and turns on the lamp that's on top. Then he walks over to his fireplace where he stokes the fire to life. Then he moves over to his bed where he takes off his shoes, slips into his pajamas and his comfortable slippers.

From the nightstand alongside his bed, he picks up his reading glasses and positions them on his head. Then he picks up his pipe and smiles.

He inserts the pipe into the corner of his mouth and lifts up a small leather sack, and then he fumbles inside for a small wad of his favorite tobacco, finding this little ball of joy, he loads his pipe with the aromatic golden glob.

Once prepared, he puts the pipe back in his mouth... unlit, and stands up, making his way to his refrigerator in his kitchenette. He gets out a bottle of milk and pours himself half a glass.

On the counter sits a plate that is covered with a clear glass dome, and under that dome is a stack of assorted cookies from his bakery downstairs.

He takes down a dish from the shelf above, and lifts the glass cover off the cookie plate... Then he methodically searches through the stack of cookies until he locates a few of his favorites and he stacks them on the dish.

Then he walks his milk and cookies over to a big, leather, wing backed chair that sits in the corner of the room next to the small round table where a little lamp is setting.

Giuseppe places the milk and cookies on a little round white doily on the table. On the doily sits a small box of matches, an ashtray, and an open book that is lying face down with its pages spread apart. Obviously the book is set so that it marks the last place Giuseppe had read to the night before, it waits patiently 'at the ready' so he can start where he last left off.

At the foot of the chair is a matching leather ottoman, and on it is a crumpled blanket.

Giuseppe scoots in between the ottoman and the chair and takes a seat; he reaches down to pull the ottoman closer, and simultaneously he lifts his feet up, covering his lower half with the blanket at the same time. He leans back into his favorite chair and speaks out of the side of his mouth where there is no pipe, and says, ***"Ahhhh, now this is the life".***

As the evening light coming in from the window transforms into darkness, Giuseppe picks up the matches and lights his pipe. He leans back puffing on it until a red-hot ember sends the aromatic smell of his favorite tobacco into a mesmerizing cloud of white smoke. The smoke seems to create a hypnotic dance upon the air. He tucks the blanket in around his waist and carefully picks up his book. For the first time we are able to read the title, and it is clear that Giuseppe is enjoying '**The Adventures of Sherlock Holmes**.'

After a few minutes of reading, Giuseppe smiles and laughs out loud, before turning the page. Obviously he is keeping himself entertained.

As the pages are turned, the night rolls on, and through the window we notice that night has finally arrived in its full glory.

The moon rises across the valley, and Giuseppe yawns, this is his natural alarm telling him that he needs to call it a day.

Sleep is now the priority he desires. Cookies and milk are a far cry from a decent dinner, but now sleep seems more important than eating. He taps his long extinguished pipe in the ashtray on the little table; then he sets his book down and stands, making his way over to his bathroom to wash up before climbing into bed.

Hidden by the evening's shadows Giuseppe gets out of his clothes and slips between the covers. Off come his glasses, and we strain to see him wind up his alarm clock. So ends another long day for Moratuzzi's most famous baker. Moratuzzi's **ONLY** baker.

The Dark Cave of Treasures

Occasionally the relative silence from upstairs is broken by a lone creak from the wooden floor in Giuseppe's apartment, which is usually followed by the faint smell of pipe tobacco. These are the signs that Watson waits for each night before he and Willie invade the bakery.

Once the snoring starts, then Watson knows that the coast is clear.

It isn't long before they are confident that they will have the run of the bakery because Giuseppe usually falls asleep quickly.

And right on schedule, the first of many low rumblings makes its way down to the lower level of the bakery. Giuseppe is finally snoring, the signal that Watson & Willie have been waiting for.

Watson reaches back behind himself and starts to motion to Willie with his outstretched paw, **"OK. The coast is clear, let's go!"**

Willie gets up off the empty spool of thread where he has been lounging and makes his way towards their front door, in an almost anti-climactic way he says, **"Finally! I've been starving for nearly an hour."**

Almost sarcastically Watson says, **"Take a look at yourself in that mirror over there. You're in no danger of starving".**

Watson swings their front door all the way open and allows Willie to walk out first. As Willie passes, Watson reminds him, **"Now, remember... Crumbs and drips, little pieces only! I don't want you to take any huge bites. Use a little finesse as you dine, so Giuseppe doesn't ever know that we were there. OK?"**

Willie looks perturbed**. "Yeah, Yeah, Yeah. I get it."**

The two mouses [sic] make their way into the dimly lit, cavernous bakery. Cavernous according to Watson & Willie.

With clean floors, the absence of Giuseppe and his customers, and the glow of a single incandescent light, the nighttime bakery is a very different place than it is during regular business hours.

Watson has often felt that the experience might be similar to entering a huge cathedral, but then again, he couldn't be sure because he was not a 'church mouse.'

Suddenly the bakery becomes a room full of scary echoes and shadows. It's a good thing that mouses [sic] have great night vision, and big floppy ears to hear each and every noise, or a mouse as skittish as Willie might never eat again.

Working together Watson & Willie climb up the back of each showcase and methodically, with each other's help, they manage to slide the showcase doors open just enough to squeeze inside where the true gold of the bakery is stored.

Giuseppe meets Double-Trouble

Watson didn't get to be as old as he is by being stupid, so after a full night of foraging with Willie, he always goes back to each and every showcase and table that they visited, to make darn sure that all traces of their mischief have been erased.

Often he has to pick up, and clean up, the mess that Willie is prone to leaving, and he credits his own diligence for keeping the two of them safe from harm.

As dawn begins to break, familiar creaks and groans begin to emanate from the wooden floors above... Giuseppe is awake! Watson knows that it won't be long before he will come downstairs and be heading for the kitchen in the bakery. The clock is ticking now, and two mouses [sic] need to be long gone before Giuseppe arrives!

Getting Willie to comply is a lot easier after he has a full tummy, than when he's hungry, so when Watson gives the high-sign, Willie reacts immediately, and the two of them skedaddle back into their little mouse-house.

Sure enough, Watson is barely in bed when they hear the familiar footsteps of Giuseppe entering the bakery's kitchen.

Pots start to clang, and faucets burst forth with clear clean water from the artesian springs in Moratuzzi, and all of this noise is occasionally accentuated by the slamming of an oven door or two.

It's a lot of noise but once safely inside their home both mice seem to drift off to sleep regardless of the distractions.

Willie starts to snore, and we can see that he has taken up the habit of stuffing his big old floppy ears with cotton balls to stifle the noise that drifts in from the bakery.

Watson seems to handle the noise from the bakery a lot better than Willie's loud snoring, but he understands that the price for a paradise like this, doesn't come cheap.

By nine am the little bell over the front door rings, signaling the first of many customers who will visit the bakery throughout the morning, and the procession of hungry villagers seems to continue throughout the rest of the day as well.

Around 11 am Anthony Stabenelli enters the bakery, with his 'more than nasty' little mutt, **Spike**, who Anthony is carrying under his left arm.

Today is a bit different as Anthony also has his two young twin nephews with him, Butch and Chester. Giuseppe comes out to his side of the showcase and smiles, ***"Anthony, how are you my friend?"***

Anthony rolls his eyes and then sets Spike down on the floor beside him. When he stands up he says, ***"Giuseppe, I can tell you, that I have been better! Today my brother has saddled me with the responsibility of supervising his two kids."***

Giuseppe tries to muster up his best concerned expression as Anthony goes on and on about how his brother's two kids really cramp his style, etc., but in reality Giuseppe really isn't listening to a word he's saying.

As Anthony and Giuseppe continue to exchange this pseudo-conversation, one of Anthony's nephews (Butch) starts to edge his way behind the showcase, but Giuseppe has learned to keep an eye on potential trouble; especially from unruly children, and he gently scoots the boy back to the proper side of the room. This he does with such finesse – that Anthony isn't even aware that it's happening.

Meanwhile the other little monster (Chester) is painting the glass in front of Giuseppe's showcase with drool mixed in with dirty hands. This he manages to do nonchalantly, as he stares at all the delicious desserts that beckon to him from the glass shelves inside.

Giuseppe, being the observant one, and hopeful to try anything that might calm these two monsters down, asks, **_"Would you two boys like to try one of my delicious custard filled pastries?"_**

The two little brats nod in unison, and Giuseppe takes a pair of tongs, opens the back of the showcase, and picks out two big custard-filled French pastries. With his free hand he grabs a couple of paper napkins.

He walks around the showcase to the customer side and squats down to the boy's level and attempts to hand the first boy a clean napkin, but the rude little brat reaches out and grabs both pastries from his other hand. Quick thinking Giuseppe snatches one back - and hands it to the second boy who grabs it like a starving animal.

Then he hands each kid a clean napkin before returning to his side of the showcase.

When Giuseppe looks back at the first boy, the kid is actually glaring at him, and he could have sworn that the kid stuck out his tongue, but even with a quick second-look, he couldn't be sure.

C.J.

Anthony smiles and says, **"Now isn't that a nice thing for Mr. Alessandro to do, can you both say thank you?"** but each kid is busy stuffing his face and neither utters a word.

About that time Spike lets out a little sad cry, and Giuseppe smiles, reaching for a small basket full of cookie samples.

He comes back around to the customer side of the showcase and bends down to pat Spike on the head. As he does, one of the twins reaches into the basket, and grabs a handful of cookies, but, without looking, Giuseppe grabs the kid by the wrist and squeezes hard, until the little thief lets go, with a shocked look on his face.

This "dance-for-control-of-the-situation" goes on without Anthony noticing a thing, or, missing a beat in his monotonous complaining. As a result, Anthony is never the wiser for what's going on between Giuseppe and Anthony's two nephews.

Meanwhile Giuseppe picks out a single cookie, and hand feeds it to Spike saying, **"There ya go little man**".

Spike's tail starts to wag, and soon his whole rear end is swinging from side to side. Spike seems to be so happy, that Giuseppe wonders how he can keep himself from falling over. Despite the fact that

Giuseppe has always hated Anthony's dog, he's suddenly made a friend.

Giuseppe sets the basket of cookies back on the top of the showcase and asks, **"So, Anthony, how can I help you?"**

Anxiously Anthony responds, **"Well... with my brother and his two brats in town, we're probably going to have to add a few extra things to my order for my upcoming event, which is coming up soon. I brought these two down here to pick out a few things that they might like, but I guess they like everything so add on a couple of everything you've got, and I'll make my brother pay for them."**

Giuseppe keeps smiling and quickly writes a few notes so he can upgrade Anthony's most recent order.

Thankfully Anthony bids him farewell, taking his brood outside.

As Giuseppe turns he notices that the cookie basket full of samples is missing. He rushes to the front window just in time to see Anthony, Spike, Butch, and Chester driving away in Anthony's car.

From the backseat the two brats are smiling as they thumb their noses towards Giuseppe, holding up the sample basket in defiance.

Donatella has met The Twins

Giuseppe begins to fume once he realizes that Anthony's two nephews have pulled the wool over his eyes. He walks to the back of the bakery to retrieve a damp cloth so he can start cleaning the messy glass on his showcases out front.

He gets to work, trying to get the sticky mess off the glass. *"Man"* he says out loud. *"Thank God those brats don't come in here every day."*

From behind him comes a soft females voice... *"Brats?"* Giuseppe is startled and actually jumps, clutching his chest. *"Oh, You startled me."* He says.

Giuseppe was apparently so caught up in his own anger, and the cleaning, that he didn't hear the bell on his front door, but there in all her beauty is Donatella. She smiles and repeats her question, *"Brats?"*

Giuseppe musters up a big smile for Donatella, and shakes his head, almost embarrassingly. *"Oh, you just missed Anthony and his nephews, they just left".*

Donatella rolls her eyes upwards and clutches her own chest. *"Those two kids are too much, aren't they? I wasn't around them for more than a few minutes and I could tell that they were trouble with a capital 'T'. I mean, I actually like children, but I would believe that I was cursed, if those two boys were mine. I truly pity their mother."*

Giuseppe, trying his best not to cast any more disparaging remarks about Anthony or his family members, quickly does his best to change the subject, *"So, how can I help you miss Donatella?"*

Donatella smiles and says, *"My mother is hosting her book club this afternoon and she'd like some of your wonderful French bread, two loaves please. And if you promise not to tell her when she comes in here, I'd like one of your custard pastries."*

She pauses. *"If you don't mind me asking, what did Anthony want?"*

"Anthony brought his nephews in here to pick out some special treats, especially for them." Giuseppe explains.

Donatella chuckled and shook her head, *"I don't know why, but I think that he hates those kids more than everyone else does."*

Giuseppe laughs and adds, *"Well, I really don't hate them. Kids are just kids, ya know?"*

She laughs. *"Oh well, I guess we shouldn't laugh at someone else's expense, especially when they aren't here to defend themselves."*

Giuseppe is dying to ask, so he finally does, *"I've seen you and Anthony riding around in his fancy car, and I assume that he's fond of you?"*

She frowns and makes a face. *"I'm sure he'd like us to be together, but... he thinks that he can get the interest of all the girls in town, just because his family has money."*

She thinks about the situation some more, and only makes herself more irritated. *"My family has money, and you don't see me carousing all over Moratuzzi with every man I meet."*

The more she explains the angrier she seemed to become. Now Giuseppe realizes that he may have struck a nerve, and he is almost sorry he asked. A little bit embarrassed, he hangs his head.

Donatella notices that he's a bit uncomfortable. *"Oh, I'm sorry Giuseppe, Anthony is kind of fun, but I can't see myself ending up with a guy like that."*

Giuseppe is thrilled to hear this news, and now for the first time since he came back to Moratuzzi he feels that there is a spark of hope.

Lessons Learned

Willie stirs from his morning slumber and spots Watson peeking out from their front door into the bakery. He rubs his eyes and yawns, **"Hey Watson, wassss up?"**

Watson closes the door and laughs. **"I was just watching Giuseppe deal with Anthony's nephews. Man, I can see what a couple of troublemakers those two kids are!"**

"Eh, they're not our problem, so who cares." Chimes Willie. **"Is there any more French bread left?"** he asks.

"Last night you ate the last of the bread" replies Watson. **"But today's the day Giuseppe gets a new load of bread making ingredients, so tonight we can replenish our pantry with fresh stuff."**

"Hummm, OK. That'll be good." Willie responds. Then he asks, *"How about pie? Do we have any more of that lemon meringue?"*

Watson puts his paws on his hips and glares at Willie. *"When did I become your waiter? Are you helpless? If you want something to eat you know where it is!"*

Willie recoils a bit, *"Geeze, I'm sorry. Who wound up your clock?"* He asks, as he makes his way over to their little kitchen area.

The kitchen is kind of a mess from their meal the night before, and as Willie get closer he starts shaking his head at the dirty dishes.

Watson sees him and makes sure to announce the facts. *"Quite a mess huh? And I'm sure you'll be shocked to know that those are all <u>your</u> dishes."*

Willie is now feeling a little bit guilty and responds, *"OK. I'll clean that up."*

Watson walks over to the book that he's been reading and takes a seat. *"I'll alert the media..."*

Willie didn't quite hear Watsons comment and asks, *"Huh?"*

Watson replies, *"Nothing."*

True to his word Willie actually does a great job of cleaning up what remained of the previous night's mess, and Watson is quite impressed.

It isn't too often that Willie pulls his own weight, but what really frustrates Watson is that he knows that when Willie FINALLY gets started, he really can do a good job. IF... he wants to. Watson settles into his book, and Willie goes back to bed.

Within a few minutes the first of many bakery supply companies arrives with part of the weekly supply of bakery goods. Baking soda, salt, and other spices, flour and large amounts of creamery butter and milk, along with some cheeses and of course caramel, butterscotch, vanilla, and squares of milk chocolate for Giuseppe's fabulous desserts.

Probably one of the most important deliveries is the ingredient that Giuseppe will need to make loaves of bread, because bread is the staple of Moratuzzi. Without bread... Giuseppe would lose his customer base.

He makes all his profits from his desserts, but the income from bread sales is what essentially keeps the doors open to his bakery. Without bread, he'd have a tough time staying open.

As a result, once he manages to create the dough for bread making, he values and protects it like gold. The mixes must be put together just right for the various types of bread, and the dough must be stored at the exact temperatures so that he has enough to make enough fresh loaves for the coming week. Once he runs out, the whole process starts all over again, week to week.

So, when Giuseppe hears the trucks arriving he always runs out back to greet the various delivery men, and he always gives them a cup of fresh coffee that he brews for this reason, and he usually adds a few cookies or a French Pastry to sweeten the gesture.

This practice has cemented wonderful relationships, with all the drivers, over time. So much so; that now, they've all become members of his extended family.

The rewards of treating each driver well, have proven themselves over the years. Especially when certain times of the year bring poor weather conditions. While other businesses complain that the drivers are lazy, or too scared to travel the mountain roads, when the weather is bad, Giuseppe's deliveries are seldom delayed for any reason.

Sunday's, after church... when local businessmen usually get together for lunch and a brief meeting to discuss local commerce, Giuseppe is often asked what his secret is to keeping the flow of 'his ingredients' coming, even in poor weather? He just smiles and says, **"You get better results with honey, than with vinegar."**

Most of the other merchants have all heard this explanation in prior years, but just about all of them are so dense that they think Giuseppe is being a wise guy, when in fact, the statement he gives, is a perfect answer to their question. Giuseppe learned early on [from his parents] that kindness is always rewarded.

Despite the presence of a few naysayers in the group of local merchants, Giuseppe is well liked by the majority of the entrepreneurs.

Naturally it did not hurt that his parents were pillars of the community long before he stepped up to the plate, but even so, his good natured demeanor has made him a very likable fellow indeed.

Peter Kowalski, who moved with his family to Moratuzzi three years ago, came all the way from Czechoslovakia, for a life in Italy.

Peter often tries to sit next to Giuseppe at the meeting of the local businessmen, and he always seems to be the most interested in picking Giuseppe's brain for ways to improve his hardware business.

Often the subject reverts to tangible merchandise, that once purchased, never seems to need to be purchased again.

Peter always tries to compare his situation to Giuseppe's bakery operation, even though their two businesses are very different.

Apparently Giuseppe's baked goods, which are consumed over and over again, each and every week, is what seems to confound Peter. Seems that he'd like that same type of business activity to happen in his hardware store.

On a number of occasions Giuseppe has tried to direct Peter to think "differently" about how he can use his "Satisfied Customer Base" to provide testimonials about well-made products to other potential customers. **New customers!**

Giuseppe tries to keep nudging Kowalski into "**selling the sense of reliability that his longtime customers seem to have**" and **not** just the products themselves. It's the reliability of those products that bring real value to the people of Moratuzzi who are very practical folks at heart.

Giuseppe explains, ***"You know Peter, selling bread isn't all that different than selling hammers."*** Kowalski looks confused.

"What I mean is, if your customer breaks a hammer, he comes in and buys a new one right?" ...Kowalski nods.

"Well, that's essentially what happens when one of my customers eats a loaf of bread. The bread is gone... just like the hammer is broken." ...Giuseppe explains.

Now Kowalski looks even more confused.

"What I'm trying to say is... <u>what if</u> your customer. The one who bought one of your great hammers," Kowalski nods... *"<u>What if</u> he told his neighbor about how great his new hammer was, and how much work he was able to produce when using it. What would happen?"*

Kowalski ponders the situation for a brief moment and then answers, *"Well, I guess his neighbor would come in and buy a hammer!"*

Giuseppe smiles and nods 'yes' while tapping his finger on his temple. And Peter smiles. Giuseppe says, *"That's right my friend. Now you've got it!"*

This milestone is Giuseppe's chance to walk away and he does. He knows that in order to make the most out of these business meetings, he needs to circulate.

Although he likes Peter, he also knows that it is unlikely that he'll be able to teach much to Mr. Kowalski. Giuseppe must be one of the most patient men in the village because he's told the hammer story to Peter several times in the past. But Peter just doesn't seem to understand.

However, when he gives it serious thought, he realizes that even though many businessmen seem to seek his help, in the end, they want to do things their own way, <u>right or wrong</u>.

Music Track: "Autumn's Last"

Unexpected Visitors

The sun has gone down and the silence of the night is rolling around. Watson, who had fallen asleep while reading his book, begins to stir from his slumber. It's almost time for hungry mouses [sic] to start foraging for food.

Watson stretches and finally stands up, bending his back by pressing his paws on his hips. Then he lets out a big yawn.

This activity [and noise] seems to get Willie's attention, and he begins to stir as well, stretching in his bed, even though he's still half asleep, he inadvertently kicks the covers off the end of the bed leaving him exposed to the cooler night air. Watson is mildly amused to watch him in his sleepy slumber, trying to reach down to grab covers that are no longer there.

Watson has a good laugh at Willie's expense, and says, **"Hey. Willie? Time to rise and shine."**

Willie sits up but it's plainly obvious that he's still in dreamland because he responds in a slurred tone, **"Is it bread day?"**

By now, Watson has regained his senses, and he's back to being 'sharp as a tack'. **"No. Not yet. Giuseppe just prepared all the dough today, then he'll bake the bread tomorrow, and tomorrow night we can feast on fresh stuff."**

Willie starts to pat his paw over his open mouth as he yawns, and simultaneously he tilts his head to one side until he ultimately falls back over, onto his bed.

He mumbles, **"OK. Wake me tomorrow when there's new bread to eat."**

Watson has seen this all before and isn't going to let Willie go back to sleep. **"No, No, No. Come on, wake up, that way you can help me gather a few morsels, because in an hour, you're going to be hungry again!"**

Willie doesn't like having to wake up, he loves sleeping. But Watson uses the opportune word...

'**hungry**', so Willie does his best to wake himself up, as he cautiously stands on his wobbly legs.

On most days Willie is anxious to get out into the bakery, as fast as possible, but on days when Giuseppe has concentrated on preparing bread dough, he isn't too overjoyed, especially when there's few crumbs to gnaw on from the day before. And yesterday Watson had found an apple out back, so at least there's something different to chew on tonight.

Willie starts to shuffle his way to the kitchen, but Watson snapped his paw and once he got Willie's attention, he points towards the bathroom, and Willie changes course so he can wash up.

We watch as Willie washes and then goes over to their little kitchen area. He grabs a big chunk of chocolate chip cookie and uses a small thimble (for a glass) so he can pour himself some milk. Then Willie walks over to where Watson is engrossed in his book. *"What's that?"*

Watson replies, *"It's a book about a famous human named Benjamin Franklin, who was sort of an inventor and statesman."*

"Statesman?" Inquires Willie. *"What's a Statesman?"*

Watson thinks about how he can present this so Willie can understand. *"Well, you know how we have rules around here? Like washing before you eat, and keeping quiet and out of sight during the day?"*

He pauses to let that sink in, and then he says, *"Well... the humans have set up governments, and one of the most famous humans who helped set up the rules for America... remember when I told you about America? Anyway, Franklin helped establish the rules for America. Benjamin Franklin was his name."* and Willie nods that he understands.

Watson continues, *"Anyway, the humans had forefathers that set up the first rules so that EVERYONE could live in an orderly fashion."*

Willie seems surprised and says, *"Gee I thought mice were bad. It's no wonder humans have lots of rules... Having 4 fathers makes for a lot of bosses!"*

Watson shakes his head because of Willies obvious misunderstanding, but after thinking it over, he decides that it's **not** worth his time to correct him.

As Willie takes a seat at their little kitchen table the room returns to silence, then, all of a sudden there's the sound of glass breaking.

Both mice are startled, and Watson hurries over to their door and peaks out into the bakery. Willie is noticeably scared and shuffles to their door directly behind Watson. He nervously asks, **"Is that the new cat?"**

Watson shrugs knocking Willie's paw off his shoulder and nudges him to step back as he feels that Willie is crowding him, and Watson doesn't want Willie hanging all over him while he's trying to listen. **"I think this is bigger than a cat."**

Soon our point of view is the bakery as if we're privy to Watson's *point of view*. It's a rather dark view of the back workroom in the bakery and hard to focus, when all of a sudden, a big shoe steps right in front of their mouse door.

Watson is startled and takes a nervous step backwards, and because Willie is standing so close, the two of them topple over each other into a heap.

Willie is scared and whispers, **"What is it? A Monster? What?"**

Watson gets to his feet and using his two paws he motions downward and says, **"Try to keep your voice down, someone just broke into the bakery, come on."** And he makes his way back over to the door that is still slightly ajar. He peeks out again.

Now it's clear, and he whispers his findings to Willie who is listening intently, **"It's those two delinquent nephews of Anthony's."**

Willie is a bit perplexed and asks, **"What do they want here, this is just a bakery"**.

In the meanwhile, the two twin brothers make their way from showcase to showcase, where they unfurl a couple of white pillowcases.

One of the brothers holds the pillowcase open, while the other slides the showcases open one at a time, scooping up cookies and cupcakes and pastries and packing them into the pillowcase.

They fill up one of the sacks, and then they set the full pillowcase aside, only to start filling the other one. All the while each boy is giggling as they start stuffing their faces like the little pigs that they are.

About ten minutes into their heist, one of the two brothers sees a note that Giuseppe had left behind for himself, which reminds him to take the bread dough out of the cooler by 11 am.

The kids don't realize the importance of the note, but they assume that this dough has some significant importance to Giuseppe. And as far as they're concerned, they wants to spoil things for Giuseppe as much as possible.

They begin to move toward the cooler, when one of the brothers inadvertently trips over the first pillowcase full of goodies. Wham, Bang, Crash, and both boys burst out into laughter. Then there's a loud creaking from Giuseppe's apartment upstairs. The two boys look at each other and the more aggressive one opens the door to the cooler and tries to lift two big cardboard boxes full of bread dough.

Bread dough is rather heavy and weighs more than this little punk thought, and he stumbles on his way out of the walk-in-cooler and drops one box.

Meanwhile the other brother kicks the pillowcase that caused his brother to stumble on, out of the way sending the stolen goods all over the bakery floor. He hoists the remaining case over his shoulder and motions for his brother to snatch one box of bread dough, and the two of them make their way towards the back door.

With one swift kick, the back door of the bakery bursts opened, and the two thieves are long gone into the cover of night. In less than a minute, Giuseppe manages to get up, and he stumbles into the bakery. He starts flipping on light switches, only to discover a chaotic mess.

A quick scan of the flour covered floor reveals that he's had at least two thieves from the white footprints all over the bakery, and he can see that his showcases have been molested, with a number of desserts removed. Then he sees it. There on the floor is the remaining pillowcase with cookies, cupcakes, and pastries spewing out all over the floor.

But the most depressing thing is that a box of bread dough has been broken open upon impact and now rests on the floor. This means that he can't use this contaminated dough for bread making. That's when he rushes to the open cooler to find that another box of bread dough is completely missing altogether. Instinctively he checks the moneybox behind the counter... but mysteriously all the money from that day's business is untouched. Now he is perplexed... **"Hummm?"**

Over the next hour or so, Giuseppe is seen mopping up the mess, throwing away any crumpled or out of place cookies, cupcakes, and pastries. Ironically there is more merchandise destroyed than there is stolen, but, losing that bread dough is really going to impact his operation for the week. He'll never be able to meet the demand of all his customers, at least not this week. Once Giuseppe gets everything nearly back to normal, he closed up the bakery for the second time, and he returns to his little apartment upstairs.

Willie is sympathetic. ***"Man, that's a tough break for Giuseppe"*** Watson is silent as he thinks things through.

Then Willie asks, ***"I wonder why those brats did that?"***

Watson is irritated, ***"They did it to be mean to Giuseppe, their meanness caused them to do this. The two of them must have been planning this since they were here the other day with their uncle Anthony"***

Willie asks, ***"I guess they don't like Giuseppe, huh?"***

Watson shakes his head and says, ***"They don't like rules, and Giuseppe was just trying to teach them that they needed to follow the rules when they're in his bakery. They didn't like Giuseppe's rules, so they wanted to get back at him."***

Willie inquires, ***"Well I guess Giuseppe will be getting a dog along with the cat, now!"***

Watson is fuming, ***"Not if I have anything to say about it! Come on, follow-me!"*** And Watson storms out of their little mouse house, straight into the bakery.

The World at the Top of the Stairs

Watson and Willie enter the bakery and Watson leads them right through the back workroom, and then through the front store portion. This he does with determination and there is no effort on his part to be quiet. Conversely Willie is trying his best to walk softly in order to keep from alerting Giuseppe, and eventually he falls behind.

Watson finally stops and turns to see where Willie is, *"Come on step it up, we ain't got all night!"*

Willie seems a little confused. *"Keep the noise down, or we'll wake Giuseppe!"*

Watson shakes his head, and slaps his own forehead, *"That's where we're headed. We're going upstairs to notify Giuseppe."*

Willie comes to a sliding stop and asks, *"Wait. For a minute there I thought that you said that we were headed upstairs to wake Giuseppe?"*

Watson looks a bit disgusted and says, *"I did! Now hurry up, will ya?"* Watson turns and resumes heading for the stairway to Giuseppe's apartment.

 "Wait, wait, what are you talking about?" Willie asks. *"When Giuseppe sees us, he's going to flip his lid! He's already in a bad mood, won't seeing*

the two of us in his bakery irritate him even more?"

Watson resumes his walking, but tries to explain... *"He can't be mad at us, cuz we didn't do this, in fact all I want to do is somehow communicate to him who actually did this."*

Willie is shocked and asks, *"You're not going to actually speak to him are you?"*

Watson is now shaking his head no. Then he says, *"No silly. We'll write him a note or something."*

Willie slows down the pace as he begins to shake his head from side to side, *"And now you're going to try to talk to a human? Why don't we just fry ourselves up and jump on a dinner plate, then he can just serve us to the new cat!"*

Watson doesn't agree, *"Oh for crying out loud, he's not interested in us at the moment. He's got bigger fish to fry."*

The two mouses [sic] make their way up the long flight of stairs to Giuseppe's front door where they pause and look at each other for a second. Willie whispers, *"Have you ever been in there?"*

Watson makes a face and motions for Willie to follow him, as he scoots under the door. But before he does he turns to Willie and adds, *"Come on, follow-me, and be careful."*

For a moment, Willie is all alone, and he speaks out loud. **_"Yeah... be careful? If there's nothing to worry about, why do I need to be careful?"_**

He musters up enough courage, and squeezes (with some difficulty) his chubby body under the small space - below the door.

Not as Scary, as We Thought

As the two mouses [sic] emerge from beneath the closed door into Giuseppe's apartment, they are both amazed how cozy Giuseppe's place really is. Against the far wall is a little fireplace and burning inside is a warm fire; that takes the chill out of the night air.

Watson immediately spots Giuseppe stretched out in a leather wingback chair, with his legs up on an ottoman. Giuseppe has a small blanket covering his feet, which are tucked in the blanket, protecting his body from the cool night air.

On his lap, face up is an open book, and that's when the two mouses [sic] are taken off guard by one of Giuseppe's huge snores. It rattles the silence of the room, but there can be no doubt that Giuseppe is still fast asleep.

Willie looks almost relieved, and whispers, **"He's sleeping."**

Watson holds his paw up to Willie's mouth, as if to remind him to be quiet. Although Willie is compelled to ask. **"I thought we didn't have to be quiet?"**

Watson hunches over and starts to move towards Giuseppe's chair. As he does, he motions with his paw for Willie to follow, and the two sneak their way over to the right side of the chair.

Watson points at Willie and motions for him to stay put, then he points first at himself and then up towards Giuseppe's lap, indicating that he's going to climb up there. Willie becomes a bit frantic and starts a silent, but nervous dance as he tries to dissuade Watson with sign language.

Watson stops, and places his paws on his hips, and gives Willie an angry look. Willie stops his crazy antics and finally shrugs his shoulders holding his paws outstretched, palms up, as if to say, 'OK. It's your funeral'.

Watson grabs onto the blanket that drapes Giuseppe and he begins the long climb up to his lap. He's timing each tug so that it corresponds with each loud snore that Giuseppe lets out.

Finally, he crests Giuseppe's lap and seems somewhat surprised that he's made it all the way to the top - without incident.

He looks cautiously back over the edge to the floor, where Willie is gawking up at his boldness.

He surveys the situation by giving Giuseppe's lap a quick three-hundred-and-sixty-degree scan. Once satisfied that the coast is clear, he cups his snout with his open paws and whispers down to Willie, **"OK. Everything looks safe."** Willie smiles and makes his way over the edge of the blanket, as if he will try to climb up next.

Watson panics a bit, and he gets Willies attention, by making a noise, "**Pssssst**" then he motions for Willie to stay put.

Then Watson disappears from Willie's view as he walks over to take a look at the book that Giuseppe is reading. He climbs up on to the lower edge and starts reading... **"Hummm, The Adventures of Sherlock Holmes"** he mutters to himself.

Being the bookworm that he truly is, he can't help himself, and soon he's reading the story, carefully turning the pages as he gets more, and more involved, pretty soon he's at the end, having lost all track of time.

Panic sets in as he remembers that Willie is still waiting down on the floor. With this in mind, he flips the back cover of the book over with some difficulty and makes his way to the edge of Giuseppe's lap.

Unfortunately, the thicker back cover is heavy duty, and makes a loud popping noise, as it slams shut on the closed book. Watson dives into the folds of the blanket to hide, as Giuseppe; understandably, stirs a bit from his slumber. Once he settles back down, Watson pops his head out and peers over the edge to a sleeping Willie, who is all curled up asleep on the edge of the blanket at floor level.

He cups his paws together and whispers, trying to wake Willie, **"Willie?"** He tries a little harder, **"Willie, wake up".**

Finally, Willie stirs, and seems to be in his usual disoriented state of mind. Watson tries getting his attention again, **"Willie, up here!"**

Willie finally remembers where he is, and as he gets to his feet, He feels the need to explain. **"Sorry... you took so long that I fell asleep. What have you been up to all this time anyway?"**

Watson responds, **"My apologies. I got caught up reading Giuseppe's book."**

Willie, because he's still half-asleep accepts Watsons excuse for a brief moment. **"Oh, you were reading,**

READING? You mean you left me down there all this time so you could read a book?"

Watson apologies, **"Look I'm sorry, but I've got an idea on how we might be able to help Giuseppe, and in doing so, maybe he and us can become friends? If we can do that, maybe he won't get that cat; and we can live here forever?"**

Willie is now just staring at Watson; his face slowly changes from expressionless to utter shock as he slowly lifts his right arm and points his paw directly at Watson and begins to shudder in fear.

Our point of view changes to Willie's, and we can see Giuseppe's head emerge behind Watson. Obviously Giuseppe has woken up, and Willie is attempting to warn Watson, so he doesn't get caught. But...

Giuseppe catches Watson by the tail, completely unaware as he picks him up for a closer look.

Watson & Willie meet Giuseppe

Watson's heart begins to pump so hard that he fears it might come flying out of his chest at any moment.

Giuseppe looks quite perturbed, as he holds Watson up to his eye level, ***"So... You want to be my friend huh?"***

Watson hangs helplessly as he realizes that he has been caught off-guard. He says, ***"You heard that?"***

Giuseppe nods very slowly and deliberately. He carefully gives Watson the evil eye, ***"If I set you down on this table will you promise not to run away?"***

Watson, looks to his left at the table top, and then back to Giuseppe's face and replies, ***"I do"*** and he raises his right arm, ***"I swear!"***

For the first time Giuseppe smiles, as he sets Watson down on the little round table next to his pipe.

Watson gathers himself up and brushes his clothing, straightening everything before making his pitch. ***"You sir, are a gentleman, and I, um, we, would like to offer our services to assist you with the***

recent break in." Watson leans in to see if Giuseppe is buying any of this.

Cautiously Giuseppe leans over the edge and looks down at the floor, placing his open right palm near Willie who is about to pee his pants.

He motions with his left finger that Willie should climb aboard, and Willie looks up to Watson who is now peering over the edge of the end table.

Watson slowly nods yes, indicating that Willie should do what Giuseppe is asking, and Willie steps aboard Giuseppe's outstretched palm for the ride up to table level, where he joins Watson.

Watson attempts to finish explaining, *"Anyway, as I was saying..."* But Giuseppe holds up his left finger to his lips as if to say, **'shush'**.

Giuseppe eyeballs Willie, pokes him in his little fat belly, and then asks, *"And who is this?"*

Watson can now see that instead of smashing these two little mouses [sic] Giuseppe is willing to talk things through.

Operating under this assumption of relative safety, he boldly steps forward and says, *"Ahhhh, this is my lifelong friend Willie, and I am Watson. I ahhhh, I have the same name as Sherlock Holmes' sidekick... that guy in the book you're reading."*

Giuseppe glances over to the book on his lap, which he notices is now closed, and he realizes he's lost track of where he had stopped reading to, which causes him to frown, as he looks back at Watson slightly irritated.

Watson immediately says, **"Page 102"**, and Giuseppe looks a bit bewildered, so Watson explains further, **"Ahhhh, that's where you left off."**

Giuseppe, is amazed at how perceptive Watson is and interrupts, **"Are all mice as smart as you are Watson?"**

Watson glances quickly over towards Willie, **"Well, not ALL mice. I'm sort of an exception."** Willie immediately starts nodding yes, as he points back towards Watson.

Watson continues, **"It's ironic, but I eh, I was just reading your book, and in some ways... Willie and I are kind of like Mr. Holmes and his sidekick."**

Giuseppe leans back in his chair and scratches his chin, **"OK. I'm listening."**

Watson steps forward, as he begins to plead his case, just like a trial lawyer. **"Well, Willie and I have certain evidence that will prove above and beyond...** Willie blurts out... **"The shadows of doubt."**

Watson knows that Willie is incorrect, but he lets this error go by without correcting him. Then Watson continues, *"Anyway, as I was saying, we have evidence, beyond the shadow of a doubt, showing who broke into the bakery tonight and stole your dough."*

Giuseppe, smirks and says, *"If you mean those footprints that were all over the bakery, I already saw them! It's plain to me that Anthony's delinquent nephews are the culprits."*

Watson raises his paw to make a point, *"Ahhhh, but that is..."* Willie interrupts Watson a second time, *"That's Circle-Stantion-Nial [sic] Evidunce."*

Watson is a bit perturbed now at Willie's interruptions. *"Willie, please. I'm trying to explain. And the word is circumstantial."*

"Anyway, what you need are eye-witnesses, and that - my dear friend - is where Willie and I come in, because we saw them with our own eyes." At this statement, Willie starts pointing his paw at his own eyes and then at Watson's, as if agreeing with his description of events.

Giuseppe rolls his eyes and says, *"Watson, please let me interrupt you for a moment. How can having you two as eyewitnesses help me? I mean, I can't pop you into my pocket and bring you down to the Constable's Office, can you imagine the look on his face when I pull out two talking mice?"*

Watson takes a seat on a box of matches on the table, he rubs his chin as he starts to consider the facts. *"Yeah, I can see how that might not turn out so good for <u>any</u> of us. However, if I learned anything from your book, all we need to do is go back and review all the evidence so we can start thinking differently about the crime. That's what Sherlock Holmes would do, right?"*

Giuseppe appreciates Watson's forward thinking, *"I must agree - Sherlock Holmes would evaluate the crime scene for the things that others miss."*

Giuseppe scoops up the two mice in his palm and says, *"Come on, let's go downstairs to see what we may have missed?"*

Half way out of the room, Giuseppe stops and looks at the two mice. He scratches his chin and stares. *"By the way do all mice talk?"*

Working the Crime Scene

So, Giuseppe, Watson and Willie all make their way downstairs to the bakery, but now they're a team. And, as they approach the bakery's workroom, Watson asks Giuseppe, **"I guess you were surprised to see us tonight, huh?"**

Giuseppe answers with confidence, **"Surprised? No. I knew the two of you were there all the time. It is just the two of you, right? Come on, let's go."**

As the three of them make their way back downstairs into the bakery, Watson rolled his eyes, and adds. **"Yeah, we're not an infestation as Anthony said the other day. So, you knew we were here all along huh?"**

Giuseppe smiles, **"I could see that you were trying really hard to cover all the evidence, but an open showcase door here, a crumb or two there, I mean, not too many things escape my eye."**

Watson gives Willie a look, **"Hummm, we'll we tried not to cause any trouble."**

Giuseppe nods in agreement. **"That's why I let you stay. The only surprise I had was that you two can talk."**

When the three of them arrived downstairs, Giuseppe walks over to the broken window and points. **"Obviously this is where they gained entry, right?"**

Watson and Willie scamper up to the counter top and look over at the broken windowpane, Watson answers, **"Yep. The two of them squeezed in; right here"**.

Giuseppe walked over to the space just in front of the cooler door and he pointed towards the floor. **"Here's where I saw all the footprints because they foolishly stepped in the flour. And over there I found a pillowcase full of goodies."**

Watson and Willie have moved to the edge of the counter and are just sitting there watching Giuseppe walk through the various parts of the crime scene, as he reenacts the crime out loud.

Watson perked up, **"It's too bad that you cleaned up the footprints; we might have gotten a print off one of their shoes. But hey, you said something about a pillowcase?"**

Giuseppe turned around and grabbed the folded pillowcase from the top of the showcase, and he lays it on the tabletop next to Watson and Willie, **"Here you go, but it's just a plain old white pillowcase.**

There's probably a hundred like that scattered all over Moratuzzi."

Watson has already begun to unfold and inspect it. *"Not like this one! Look at these embroidered initials... A. S. S., which stands for Anthony S. Stabenelli."*

Giuseppe rushes over to pick up the pillowcase smiling, then he crumples the pillowcase and tosses it back onto the counter. *"That's good Watson, but not good enough. It just proves that Anthony Stabenelli owns this pillowcase, but it doesn't prove his nephews broke in."*

Willie chimes in, *"That's some more of that 'Circle-Stantion-Nial' evidunce, for sure*!" Watson gives Willie a dirty look, and Willie reacts, *"Sorry."*

Watson begins to scratch his chin... then Giuseppe speaks, *"No. What we need is some solid proof that those two brats were here tonight!"*

Just then Watson spots a flour footprint on the back door, where the two delinquents kicked the door open to make their escape, *"Hey look, and he points. There's your evidence!"*

The three of them all look at each other with glee. There in all its glory is a footprint where one of the crooked nephews kicked the back door open.

"That's the 'smoking gun' that we've been looking for." Watson explains, *"And the good news is that all you need to do is bring the constable down here and show that to him. He'll take a picture and when he checks out the twin's shoes against that photograph... BINGO."*

Giuseppe smiles and says, *"Doctor Watson, I think you've got it!"*

Enter the Constable

It's a bright sunny morning and we see that Donatella is headed for the bakery. She has a bounce in her step, and she seems anxious to arrive.

As she reaches the doorknob to enter, she discovers that it's locked. *"My that's unusual, Giuseppe is such an early bird,"* she mutters to herself. Then she spots a small note explaining that Giuseppe will return shortly.

Just then Giuseppe actually does arrive, *"Hello Miss Donatella, I'm sorry to have kept you waiting. I was over at the constable's office, but ahhhh, I'm here now, so how can I help you."* By this time Giuseppe has retrieved his key, opened the front door, and pulled up all the shades. He steps behind the counter and smiles.

Donatella becomes a bit shy as she attempts to explain her presence, *"Well, I was in the neighborhood, and just wanted to stop by to tell you what a success my mother's book club meeting was yesterday. And... That the ladies all loved your wonderful desserts; your pastries were really the 'stars of the afternoon'!"*

Giuseppe is pleased to hear this compliment, and gives her a great big smile, but Donatella notices that Giuseppe's attention is directed to the front door. He holds up a single digit as if to say, 'please hold that thought', and he steps from behind the showcase and walks over to the front door of the bakery. In walks the constable with a clipboard and pencil.

"Good morning Mr. Alessandro." he tips his hat to Donatella and adds, *"Miss Donatella."* He looks back at Giuseppe and asks, *"Maybe you can show me how the thieves got in last night?"*

Giuseppe smiles and escorts him towards the back of the bakery. In the meanwhile, Donatella just follows the two men, as she is overcome by curiosity.

Giuseppe begins his story. *"Last night I was napping, probably around 1 or 2 am, and I heard some noise in the bakery. So, I came down to investigate, and found a huge mess. All my showcases were open and most of my goods scattered all over the floor. That's when I noticed that my cooler door was wide open too, and two boxes of bread dough were missing. I routinely use the bread dough every week so that I have the necessary ingredients to bake bread for all my customers as the week marches on. I really depend on that dough, but now I will be short on my bread deliveries."*

The constable is writing on his clipboard, he stops and looks at Giuseppe, ***"How did the thief get in?"***

Giuseppe corrects the constable, ***"Thieves, there were at least two of them!"***

The constable gets an intensive look on his face and brings up the clipboard to write and says, ***"OK. Then you were an eye witness?"***

Watson who has been peeking out of their little mouse-door all this time mutters, ***"Careful Giuseppe, careful, don't say it, don't tell him."***

Giuseppe drops his hands as if partially defeated, ***"Ahhhh, well no. Actually, I didn't see them myself."***

The constable looks a bit perplexed and asks, ***"OK. Then who saw them?"***

Giuseppe looks over towards the mouse-hole; then back to Donatella, who for lack of a better answer shrugs her shoulders, as if to say, sorry, *I can't help you*.

Then he says, **"Well, I saw a bunch of footprints' here on the floor, and they were obviously not from one person, so that's what I meant when I said that there were more than one of them."**

Watson smiles and whispers under his breathe, **"Well done old boy!"**

The constable looks down at the clean floor and asks, **"And where are they now? The footprints, that is?"**

Giuseppe smiles trying to change the subject, **"Ahhhh, here is where they broke into the bakery."** And he points at the broken window."

Then he smiles even bigger and turns around pointing at the back door. **"And... here is where they kicked the door open to make their escape."**

The constable moves closer to the rear door to take a look, as Giuseppe continues. **"There, that footprint. Can you see that? That wasn't there yesterday."**

The constable seems to be overjoyed by this new piece of evidence. He looks at Giuseppe as if to say, now were getting someplace. **"Ahhhh, this is great.**

I can take a photograph of that shoe print and when we find a match, we'll have your thief."

Giuseppe is noticeably excited that finally the constable seems to be showing some enthusiasm, as he corrects him. *"Thieves".*

The constable smiles at Giuseppe. *"Well, we don't know if there were more than one of them yet, right? Let's see if my investigation can prove that first, before we start accusing everyone in town."*

Giuseppe sheepishly smiles, and then perks up, *"Oh, and then there's this!"* and he hands the constable the pillowcase.

The constable takes the pillowcase from Giuseppe. He sets the clip board down on the counter top and stretches the pillowcase out between his two hands - looking at the monogram. He asks, *"ASS?"*

"No. No. It's his initials, A.S.S., Anthony S. Stabenelli" Giuseppe responds.

The constable scrunches up his eyebrows and asks, *"Now Mr. Alessandro you're not trying to tell me that Mr. Stabenelli broke into your bakery, and stole some bread dough, are you?"*

Suddenly Donatella who has said nothing up until now, speaks up. *"Eh Hum. Excuse me constable, but I don't believe Giuseppe is trying to blame*

103

Anthony, but Anthony's twin nephews are here in Moratuzzi visiting, and they have already proven that they are a handful. In fact, if you ask me, they're just juvenile delinquents."

She realizes that the constable isn't paying too much attention to what she has to say as a bystander, and she finally steps back.

The constable says, **"I see, well... I'll take what you said into consideration."**

Giuseppe comes to her aid. **"She's right constable, they were here in my bakery recently, and I caught them trying to sneak into my showcases, and before they left with their uncle, they actually stole my basket of samples."**

The constable closes up his clipboard and smiles. **"Well, that's hardly a major offense, but eh, OK. I'll get a copy of that footprint, and I'll pay a little visit to the Stabenelli's and those two kids, to see what we can find out. May I take that pillowcase as evidence?"**

Giuseppe gives him half a smile and nods. **"So, what's the next step?"**

The constable is walking towards the back door and looks back at Giuseppe. **"I'll get a copy of this footprint and from that I think we can straighten this out for you Mr. Alessandro."**

Giuseppe isn't smiling now as he senses that his case might be mired in bureaucratic red tape, and besides there was no telling how long Anthony's nephews would be in town.

Donatella steps up to Giuseppe and puts a warm hand on his back. ***"Don't worry, these things have a way of working out. Well, I have to run along, so I'll see you next time, OK?"***

Giuseppe smiles at her and she gives him a hug. This is the first time she has ever shown this level of affection towards him, and for a moment he almost forgets about the whole robbery.

Donatella barely closes the front door behind herself when the constable returns from the back workroom with his camera, where he took a photograph of the shoe print on the back bakery door. ***"OK. Mr. Alessandro, I'll see you next week."***

However, Giuseppe is off in a fantasy world with only Donatella on his mind and is barely cognizant of the constable's departure. He's on automatic when he responds, ***"Yeah, see ya."***

Donatella the Detective

Donatella arrives at the Stabenelli estate and knocks on the front door. In a moment a well-dressed housekeeper answers. *"May I help you Madame?"*

Donatella smiles and says, *"Yes I'm here to see Anthony Stabenelli please."*

The housekeeper asks, *"And who shall I say is calling?"*

Donatella smiles again, and replies, *"Yes, I eh, I'm Donatella Figossa".*

The housekeeper nods and says, *"One moment please..."* and she gently closes the door part way.

Donatella turns around and surveys the Stabenelli estate while she waits, and it is truly beyond belief, obviously there is wealth in this long established family.

Footsteps start to emanate from inside and they grow louder as they come closer to the front door. Then the door swings open and there stands an overjoyed Anthony, *"Donatella, my, my, I am truly surprised... what brings you all the way up here to see me?"*

Donatella has a serious look on her face. *"Anthony are you aware that your nephews were out last* evening gallivanting around town, and up to no good?"

Anthony chuckles, *"I'm sorry but that's hardly possible, we put both of them to bed early last night".*

Donatella leans forward and says, a little bit sarcastically, *"Are you sure they stayed in bed all night?"*

Anthony starts to look concerned and scratches his chin, *"What is this all about?"* he asks.

She looks sternly at Anthony, *"Last night Giuseppe's bakery was broken into, and he has good reason to suspect your nephews."*

Now Anthony takes on a carefree pose (almost defensive) and smiles at Donatella. *"Well, with all due respect Donatella, I am sure that it wasn't my nephews. They may be a handful, but thieves they are not."*

She can see that he's being difficult, and he asks, *"Are you absolutely sure about this?"*

Just then the constable's car arrives, he parks, and walks up to the front door. He tips his hat towards Donatella who smiles back at him, and he addresses Anthony, *"Good afternoon, Mr. Stabenelli I presume?"*

Anthony smiles, and responds, *"Good afternoon constable, how can I help you?"*

The constable maintains his cool composure and asks, *"Are your nephews home?"*

Anthony seems a bit shaken, and nervously replies, *"They are, but they are both in bed with stomach aches, seems they got into some of our candy and sweets and made themselves sick."* He nervously laughs.

Donatella can hardly stand his insistence to cover for these two juvenile delinquents and she chimes in, *"Ah ha... well I think that the desserts they stole from Giuseppe's Bakery is what made them sick!"*

Anthony takes a defensive posture; he raises an eyebrow, and steps closer to Donatella's face to make a point, as he comes to the aid of his nephews. *"You can't prove that! So far this is all just conjecture!"* He is obviously upset at her accusations.

The constable clears his throat to protest Donatella's interruption, and he holds up a finger to stifle her future comments. *"Ahem... Mr. Stabenelli... do you have linen pillowcases with the monogram A.S.S. on them?"*

Anthony seems surprised that the constable would know this. *"Why yes, I do but..."*

The constable reaches behind his back and reveals the pillowcase, holding it out to Anthony. Anthony takes it and lets it unfold revealing the personalized monogram. He is shocked to see that this is indeed one of his pillowcases.

He says in disbelief, *"Well, there is no doubt that this is indeed mine. But maybe Giuseppe is trying to frame me?"*

Donatella stomps her right foot at the thought that Giuseppe might be trying to frame Anthony, and besides... she knows that this isn't about Anthony (what an egotist she thinks) this is about his nephews.

The constable senses that this isn't going well between Donatella and Anthony and he quickly interrupts. *"Look Mr. Stabenelli. I also have this shoe print."* And the constable reveals a photograph that he took of the shoe print.

The constable smiles, and gently explains, *"You see, last night... obviously sometime after you put the children to bed, they must have snuck out of the house and went downtown to Giuseppe's Bakery and broke in to vandalize his shop."*

He continues. *"It is my assumption that they borrowed a couple of your pillowcases from the bedroom in order to carry the things that they planned to steal."* Anthony is in shock. The constable seems to have the entire crime all worked out.

The constable continues, *"Then they rummaged through Giuseppe's showcases filling up the pillowcases with desserts. At some point they opened his cooler and took out a couple of boxes of bread dough, and as they struggled with those, they left one of the pillowcases behind. I would guess that's when they heard Giuseppe who came down to investigate the noise."*

Anthony responds in shock, *"Oh my lord. I found a box of bread dough in the garage this morning and I wondered where that came from."*

Now Anthony is nodding in agreement with everything the constable is saying, and he looks to Donatella for forgiveness because he tried to cover for the two brats. Now he can see that he was wrong.

She realizes what he's been trying to do, and she immediately turns away from the doorway and stares out to the estate grounds, not wanting anything to do with him. He realizes that his nephews are guilty, and he also realizes that he has angered Donatella. Possibly irreparably.

He turns to the constable and asks, **"Did they cause much damage?"**

The constable tries to muster up a reassuring smile to soften the blow but realizes that he has to deliver the bad news as facts, and he explains, **"Well, they** *broke a window to gain entry, then they nearly emptied Giuseppe's showcases stealing his cookies, pastries, and cupcakes, but according to him, the worst thing is that they stole at least two boxes of bread dough from the bakery cooler and they left one on the floor, and now it's ruined."*

Anthony tries to nod reassuringly to the constable. He says, *"I will pay for all the damages constable, just tell me how much everything amounts to?"*

The constable smiles, and says, *"Well, then I will assume that this case can now be closed, right?"*

Anthony nods sheepishly, and the constable adds, *"And I further trust that you will visit Mr. Alessandro this afternoon and settle up with him? Can I trust you to do that sir?"*

Anthony nods in agreement. He notices that Donatella is walking away, and he yells, *"Donatella, hold on for a moment...?"*

Donatella doesn't even look back; as she makes a gesture with her hand, as if to say, we're done here. Anthony seems disappointed, and then regains his composure to continue with the constable.

"So, are they under arrest?" Anthony asks.

The Constable smiles. *"Well, now that the crime is solved, and we know that restitution will be made. I don't think that there's any reason to escalate things any further. Perhaps their sour stomachs will be enough punishment?"*

The constable turns to step down off the porch and then he turns back and says, *"And I would guess that once the damages are taken care of, it's unlikely that Giuseppe will press charges. You know he's a very fair-minded fellow and doesn't seem prone towards seeking revenge."*

He pauses, *"If I were you, I would show some humility when you see him this afternoon and I'd apologize on behalf of your nephews."* Anthony seems eager to comply.

The constable shifts to a slightly worried face and asks, *"So how long will your nephews be in Moratuzzi?"*

Anthony rolls his eyes and replies, *"Trust me, once they recover... I'll have them on a train back home within hours."* The constable smiles at hearing this news, as he knows that this will be the end of their shenanigans, which will make his job a lot easier.

The constable heads to his car, and Anthony closes the door and heads upstairs to show the two brats the crumpled pillowcase, and the photograph of the shoe print.

Down the hill a little way from the Stabenelli estate, the constable spots Donatella who is walking back towards town.

He pulls to the side of the road just in front of her and reaches over to open the passenger door, **"Jump in and I'll give you a lift."**

Donatella climbs aboard, and the constable can see that she is visibly upset. He assesses the situation just like any good detective and says, **"You kind of like him don't you?"**, she scowls at him and says... **"Did you see the monogram on his pillowcase? Well, that's what he is."** They both share a good laugh.

The constable smiles and says, **"I was referring to Giuseppe**."

Donatella says, **"Oh"** and she smiles but admits nothing.

The Apology, and Some Better News

Within an hour Anthony's big car pulls up out front of Giuseppe's bakery and Anthony steps inside, with his stinky dog 'Spike' in tow.

He seems quite a bit different, and not his usual pretentious self. There's no fake accent, and he's holding his open palm up to Giuseppe as he hangs his head in shame. Spike makes an attempt to run behind the showcase, and Anthony jerks his leash and points, he says, ***"Sit right down there and stay... and behave!"*** Giuseppe is stunned to see Anthony finally taking charge of his mutt!

Anthony speaks, ***"I want you to know that I am so, so, sorry about what my nephews did last night. I have come to apologize for their misbehavior, and to pay for all the damages."***

Giuseppe smiles and picks up a piece of paper where he has compiled all the damages to the penny, ***"Well I was just going to give this to the constable, but if you're willing to take care of it, then I guess we can settle this between us."***

Anthony smiles and immediately draws out his overstuffed wallet. He looks at the huge tally and makes a face... ***"Hummm looks like they really made a mess of things. Again... I'm very sorry."*** and Anthony immediately counts out a number of bills to pay the debt off.

He spots a notation on the second page, about the bread dough, ***"What about this bread dough?"*** he asks.

Giuseppe rolls his eyebrows and says, **"Oh that. I get one delivery per week from my suppliers, and from those ingredients I make the bread dough that I use to bake the bread for all my customers for the entire week. But that's gone now, and I won't be able to sell bread until my next delivery, so I'm out that income."**

Anthony is scratching his chin, **"OK, how about this? I'll pay you whatever it costs to have your ingredients delivered for, say... the next four weeks!"** He pauses and observes that Giuseppe is thinking about this.

Then he continues, **"And I'll even pay you whatever it costs to have your delivery kids visit each and every customer, to explain what happened. How's that?"**

"Anthony you don't have to do that" ...Giuseppe says.

Anthony chimes in, **"I insist, it's the least I can do before I ship those two brats back home where they belong. Eh, assuming you're not going to press charges?"**

"Now that I've cleaned up the place and calmed down a bit, no. No charges will be filed." explains Giuseppe.

Anthony reverts back to a remorseful face, *"I just wish I could fix the damage I've done regarding Donatella."*

Giuseppe perks up at hearing her name, and asks, *"Donatella?"*

Anthony continues, *"Yes. When the constable came out to my home this morning, Donatella was already there speaking to me about the break in, and I don't know why I just didn't believe her, and I started sticking up for my nephews instead. Then the constable showed up with that photo of the foot print and my pillowcase, and... Well... you can imagine how stupid I felt?"*

Giuseppe mumbles... *"Why yes. I can imagine how stupid you are, eh... were, sorry."*

Anthony doesn't quite hear Giuseppe and asks... *"Huh?"*

Giuseppe smiles and says... *"Nothing, go on."*

Anthony continues, *"Anyway, I was kind of getting to like Donatella, but now... I don't think that she'll ever speak to me again. "*

Then without warning Anthony seems to backslide into his predictable self-absorbed personality and he comments, *"But there are a lot of other fish in the sea, so I guess I'll just have to move on?"*

Giuseppe, after hearing this news, is beside himself with glee, and without thinking he says, ***"I think that's the best idea that you've ever had Anthony!"***

After receiving Giuseppe's approval, Anthony smiles and replies... ***"By golly, I think you're right!"*** As he turns to leave the bakery, the door opens and in steps Donatella.

Anthony gives her a rude stare, and as he passes her, he stops deliberately to say, ***"Hummm",*** then he storms out of the bakery, climbs into his car, and drives off.

Donatella carefully closes the front door to the bakery, and she turns towards Giuseppe, ***"I can't believe that TWIT is actually mad at ME... how obnoxious!"***

Giuseppe is smiling from ear-to-ear like a Cheshire cat, but otherwise he is struggling not to laugh out loud.

After shutting the front door that Anthony left open, she walks the short distance from the front door to the showcase and says to Giuseppe, ***"I say... good riddance!"***

Curiosity seems to overtake her now, ***"So did that cretin stick up for those two little troublemakers?"***

Giuseppe still smiling reaches down behind the showcase and pulls out a huge wad of money, *"No. Actually, he came to make amends, and then some."*

Donatella smiled and then said, *"Well you won't see that every day, it's truly a miracle isn't it?"*

Giuseppe smiled and added, *"And the day is just beginning. Want to see another miracle?"*

Donatella's curiosity is unleashed as she senses that Giuseppe is about to reveal a secret. Giuseppe walks to the front of the bakery and locks the door, and then he pulls down the shades. Donatella is bewildered but stays with him because she is curious.

Giuseppe says, *"Are you afraid of mice?"*

Donatella says, *"Afraid? Well, not exactly afraid... but ahhhh..."* she pauses for more of Giuseppe's story, when he interrupts, *"Good! I want to show you something."*

He uses his index finger to entice her into the backroom, and she follows. Then he bends over a bit and faces the little door on the mouse hole.

He says, *"Boys?"*

He waits a second*, "Come on now, you two, I want you to meet someone who is very special to me."*

He pauses and then says, **"Watson? And you too Willie, come out of there right now! She can be trusted!"**

Very slowly the front door to the little mouse house begins to creak open, and out step the two little rascals.

Donatella now has a surprised look on her face. Obviously she doesn't know what to make of this, and she looks towards Giuseppe for a reasonable answer. Giuseppe laughs, **"They're kind of cute aren't they?"**

She starts to break into a very big smile and begins to nod in agreement, **"Why yes, I guess. Yes. They are indeed!"**

Giuseppe giggles, and then looks back towards the mice. Now he reaches his hands down towards them and curls his fingers to and fro as if to ask them to 'step aboard'.

Willie is bewildered and looks at Watson, and Watson shakes his head! Then Willie looks at Giuseppe and starts moving his paws in the air as if he's already protesting what Giuseppe wants them to do next.

Giuseppe rolls his eyes, and stands up putting his hands on his hips, **"Come on Fellas, we can trust Donatella."**

120

Watson steps forward and says, **"OK. But she's the only one, promise?"** Giuseppe starts nodding in agreement. Donatella actually hears Watson speak and she is speechless, as she points at him, **"He ahhhh, He ahhhh..."**

Then she starts to faint, and Giuseppe catches her and helps to get her seated on a stool.

Once she is comfortably seated Giuseppe laughs, and confirms it, **"Yes, they talk."** Donatella puts her hand over her mouth as she can hardly contain herself from screaming in amazement.

Music Track: "Falling in Love"

Love Conquers All

Narrator: *All that winter, Donatella and Giuseppe were inseparable, and as the seasons moved into spring the warm weather came back around, and by then cupid had shot enough arrows into Donatella and Giuseppe's hearts that they found themselves deeply in love.*

In May they were married, and after the minister pronounced them man and wife they had their first kiss.

Giuseppe smiled and pulled the edge of his breast pocket open as he looked down to reveal that Watson and Willie were there for the entire event. He winked at both of them; because by that time they had become close friends, as both of them smiled back.

C.J.

And that is how two mouses [sic], and the finest couple in the bakery business, became an absolutely wonderful family.

Oh, and the cat? Well, they never did get a cat.

THE END

122

Track: "Tarantella Celebration"

About the Author...

DENNY MAGIC

IF YOU HAVE ANY INTEREST IN MY LIFE STORY... PLEASE VISIT MY WEBSITE AT DENNYMAGIC1.COM, AND NAVIGATE OVER TO MY "BIO" PAGE WHERE YOU CAN FIND MY 500 PAGE AUTOBIOGRAPHY.

Denny Magic
Published writer

more than 40 short stories published with Amazon.com as of 2023

www.dennymagic1.com

Audio Versions available from Audible.Com

Walking with Walt

one man's journey in the footsteps of Walt Disney

by Denny Magic

About the Composer...

Scottish born Tom Rae lives in Dunoon, Argyll, Scotland. Tom has been making music contributions to projects created by Denny Magic since 1996. First with The Franchesa Group, Inc. and then with Denny Magic Studios.com.

Denny considers Tom his most prolific composer and arranger, and he is considered the "go to guy" for original movie music. Tom wrote the forty-five song music score for the original "Pirates of the Caribbean" spec script entitled; "One-Eyed-Jack - The Divinity of Sonada", which is under-consideration as episode #6, over at Disney®.

Tom has written music scores for television (worldwide), and is a major contributor to 'Music Banks' who broker his music to entertainment producers' throughout Europe, and North America.

124

About the Illustrator

Cyril Jordan

Artist - Musician - Composer - Magician, and leader of San Francisco's famous Rock & Roll Band-"The Flamin' Groovies". He's currently touring the world with his rock band.

In the mid-1980's Cyril took a break from music and worked for The Walt Disney Corporation producing Mickey Mouse® comic book covers for Gladstone Comics®.

Cyril has known Denny Magic since attending grammar school together in San Francisco, California. Both men are very pleased to have remained close friends ever since. They're grateful to have an opportunity to be working together on brand-new projects.

About the Narrator...

Phil Williams
Professional Voice Talent

✔ Audible Approved
NARRATOR

Phil's Voice Overs®
1421 Sunrise Drive · Gilroy · CA · 95020
(408) 767-0135
phil@philsvoiceovers.com
www.philsvoiceovers.com

EPILOG

In late **2021** I made a sizable donation to one of George Clooney's preferred charities. I sent my money off to his Charitable Organization and NEVER expected to hear another word.

Months later I received an email that included the photograph that appears above.

Of course I was flabbergasted and I immediately tried to respond with a resounding **THANK YOU**...

However, the email that I received was a "**NO REPLY**" email address, and my reply simply bounced back as undeliverable.

That's when I decided that it must have been a **HOAX** from one of George's staff members who probably used Photoshop® to create the final picture.

It certainly did have a <u>huge effect on my psyche</u>, and as a result of my personal suspicions... I NEVER tried to incorporate the picture in any of my book advertising. I assumed that it simply was not possible that the film star **George Clooney** would be sending an unknown guy like Denny Magic, anything!

Friends who knew how hard I have been struggling to become an author kept encouraging me to, ***"Go ahead and use the photograph"***. But, no offense to my close knit buddies...

I was reluctant... seeing as I am **<u>NOT</u>** personal friends with Mr. Clooney, and I am quite sure that he doesn't know who the hell I am? And I tried to tell everyone that I didn't want to have Mr. Clooney drag me into court.

I simply could not afford for that to happen. I don't have a "Pot to pee in, or a window to throw it out of!"

Furthermore, I assumed that he **NEVER** read a single word from my "Watson & Willie" series. Him and his wife do not have children, and it was unlikely that **George Clooney** ever muttered my name.

> *I had a graphics friend of mine examine the file, and she told me that the book covers were indeed added to an existing photograph of Mr. Clooney (who was actually holding that white placard) and 'yes' it was probably created using PhotoShop®.*
>
> *She said that Mr. Clooney is actually holding a white sign in the original photo... BUT... I seriously doubt if he authorized anything to do with my children's books.*

I concluded that a staff member who works for Mr. Clooney may have taken a look at my ***sizable donation*** and decided that I might get a kick out of seeing something like this.

So I concluded that I may be the victim of a doctored photo. Regardless, I (like most of my close friends) still found the picture compelling. Which does bring me to another important aspect of my story.

It is ironic... that the following story is accurate.

As a young man, I was a co-owner of **Mah'Jek Talent Agency** in Fremont, CA.   One day I was handed the telephone number for the comedienne **Henny Youngman**, and I called Mr. Youngman in New York so I could find out how I might be able to assist him.

Mr. Youngman enjoyed an illustrious career in movies in the 1920's and 1930's. Later he appeared on television on shows like The Milton Berle Show and Syd Caesar's Comedy Hour.

I was thrilled to be speaking with a legend, and we talked for more than an hour.

During that call he told me how he was friends with **Rosemary Clooney** (*George Clooney's Aunt*), and he wondered if my talent agency could help her in some way to get back to work.

She had just released a book and he told me that she'd like to, "***Get back in the swing of things***", and he asked me to contact her with my thoughts.

He added the comment, *"Yes she was 'over the hill, like himself, but she asked him as a personal friend, to help her get back to work".*

There was no way that my current customer base would listen to me pitching an entertainer who was a popular singer and actress from a bygone age.

By the time I was booking entertainers everything was modernized to the point that 'Rock and Pop' were the top requests.

I tried to explain that in order to be able to place **Rosemary** ANYPLACE was BEYOND my capability.

But **Mr. Youngman** said, ***"Well, at least call her and let her know what kind of obstacles you're facing. At least a courtesy call would be*** *appreciated, I'm sure.*" And he gave me Rosemary Clooney's telephone number.

Number one, I was amazed that I actually had a chance to speak with the famous **Henny Youngman**.

Number two, I did called **George Clooney's Aunt** and we chatted for almost an hour. I could sense in her voice that all she wanted to do was get back to work. So I was as gentle (and courteous) as I possibly could have been, as I tried to explain how the business had changed and that the market was not open minded enough to allow me to make those vital connections for her. She seemed greatly disappointed. I can relate, when I compare my own struggles as an unknown author.

She was greatly disappointed and I actually felt bad that I was not going to be able to help her attain her goals. I wished I could have helped her. As I write this, I realize that George Clooney will never know how I had been touched by him, and his father along with his aunt.

Funny how the world is, huh? Our paths can cross without some of us ever knowing what actually happened. Someday I hope that **George** and me can share a laugh over this.

Made in the USA
Middletown, DE
26 January 2025

70260810R00080